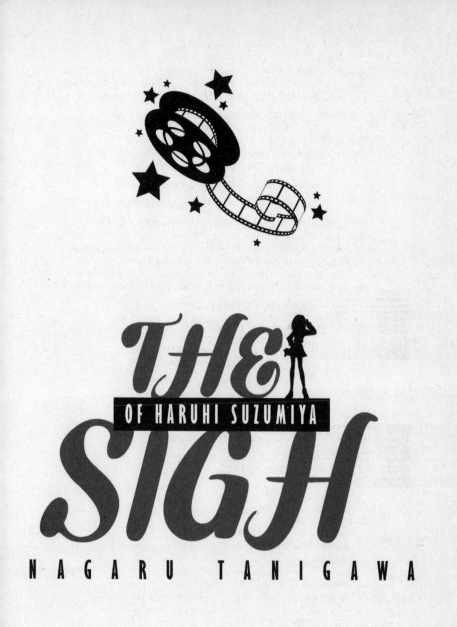

THE SIGH OF HARUHI SUZUMIYA

NAGARU TANIGAWA

Edited by KADOKAWA SHOTEN
First published in Japan in 2003 by KADOKAWA CORPORATION, Tokyo
English translation rights arranged with KADOKAWA CORPORATION, Tokyo, through TUTTLE-MORI AGENCY, INC., Tokyo.

English translation by Chris Pai for MX Media LLC

Little, Brown and Company

Hachette Book Group
237 Park Avenue, New York, NY 10017
Visit our Web site at www.lb-teens.com
www.jointhesosbrigade.com

Little, Brown and Company is a division of
Hachette Book Group, Inc.
The Little, Brown name and logo are
trademarks of Hachette Book Group, Inc.

First U.S. Edition: October 2009

Library of Congress Cataloging-in-Publication Data

Tanigawa, Nagaru.
[Suzumiya Haruhi no tameiki. English]
The sigh of Haruhi Suzumiya / by Nagaru Tanigawa; illustrations by Noizi Ito. —1st ed.
p. cm.
Summary: The SOS Brigade decides to make a movie starring the club's members, but it seems as though Haruhi is causing the plot elements of the film to really happen.
ISBN 978-0-316-03881-2 (hc) / 978-0-316-03879-9 (pb)
[1. Supernatural—Fiction. 2. Clubs—Fiction. 3. Video recordings—Production and direction—Fiction.] I. Ito, Noizi, ill. II. Title.
PZ7.T16139Si 2009
[Fic]—dc22

2008054397

10 9 8 7 6 5

RRD-C

Printed in the United States of America

THE SIGH OF HARUHI SUZUMIYA

NAGARU TANIGAWA

First released in Japan in 2003, *The Melancholy of Haruhi Suzumiya* quickly established itself as a publishing phenomenon, drawing much of its inspiration from Japanese pop culture and Japanese comics in particular. With this foundation, the original publication of each book in the Haruhi series included several black-and-white spot illustrations as well as a four-page color insert—all of which are faithfully reproduced here to preserve the authenticity of the first-ever English edition.

PROLOGUE

The sole worry of Haruhi, who looked like she didn't have a worry in the world, could be summed up with the words "the world was too normal."

So what would she consider "not normal"? That could be summed up in one word: "supernatural." Her mind was constantly asking, *Why hasn't a single ghost shown up before me yet?*

Incidentally, you can interchange "ghost" with "alien," "time traveler," or "esper." But as you should already know, those things only show up in fiction, not reality. Which means that Haruhi's source of distress would remain as long as she lived in this world — at least that's how it was originally. But I am currently troubled by the fact that I can no longer be so sure.

For I happen to know an alien, a time traveler, and an esper.

"Haruhi, I have something important to tell you. Listen to me."

"What?"

"You wanted aliens, time travelers, and people who could use ESP, right?"

"Yeah. What about it?"

"So, the goal of this SOS Brigade thing is to find those kinds of people, right?"

"Just finding them isn't enough. We have to have fun with them. It would feel like something was missing if we just found them and that was that. I want to be a participant, not an observer."

"I'll take being an observer for the rest of my life . . . or, yeah, moving on. An alien, a time traveler, and an esper are actually closer than you might think."

"Heh. Who might that be? I'm guessing you don't mean Yuki, Mikuru, and Koizumi, right? That wouldn't be 'closer than I might think' in the least bit."

"Uh . . . yeah . . . Actually, that's what I was about to say."

"Are you stupid? Like it would just happen to work out that way."

"Well, under normal circumstances, yeah."

"So? Who's the alien?"

"You'll love this. Yuki Nagato is an alien. Or technically, she's, uh, what? The over-something or other . . . or was it the data-mind-brain thingy? Well, some kind of alien consciousness along those lines sent her. Yeah, she's a humanoid interface. That's what it was."

"Hmm. And? What about Mikuru?"

"Asahina is quite simple to explain. She traveled through time from the future, so she's a time traveler."

"How many years into the future is she from?"

"I don't know that. She wouldn't tell me."

"Aha. I get it now."

"You do?"

"Which means Koizumi is an esper? That's what you were about to say?"

"That is in fact what I was about to say."

"I see."

And with that, Haruhi's eyebrows began twitching. She then slowly took in a deep breath before shouting.

"Don't mess with me!"

As you can see, Haruhi didn't believe the truth I'd revealed to her in the least. I guess it can't be helped. In fact, I still find it hard to believe that they're a pseudo-alien, a time traveler, and an esper freak, even after witnessing concrete proof. Asking Haruhi to believe me when she hasn't witnessed anything would be kind of a stretch.

But still, what else could I say? Every word I spoke was true. Hard as it may to be to believe, I have a habit of telling the truth when lying won't accomplish anything.

Though I'm pretty sure that if some nice person were to come up to me and start off with, "These people you know really well are actually . . . ," I would respond, "Don't mess with me!" And if that person was serious about it, I'd have to wonder if he was afflicted by some mental disease or if some freakish vibes had gotten to his head. I might even feel sorry for the guy. In any case, I'd try to avoid any contact with him.

Hmm? Wouldn't that "guy" be me right now?

"Kyon. Listen very carefully."

Haruhi glared at me with her eyes on fire.

"You're not going to find aliens, time travelers, and espers just standing around! They're so rare that we have to look for them, find them, capture them, grab them by the neck, and tie them up nice and tight so they can't get away! There is no possible way that all the brigade members I randomly chose could be that special!"

Your sentiment is absolutely correct. But count me out. The other three members are, in fact, supernatural phenomena. I am the only one who's an ordinary member of the human race that evolved on this planet. And yeah, she really did choose them randomly.

But why did this girl suddenly have common sense at such an odd time? If she had just believed me, things would be a lot simpler now. At the very least, the twisted organization known as the SOS Brigade would be able to disband. Given that it's some strange association that exists for Haruhi to find aliens (et cetera) and other mysterious things. Once she's found them, it'll no longer be needed. Haruhi can have fun with them by herself afterward. Just let me join in every once in a while. I'm fine with filling the role of the assistant on a quiz show who stands next to the host and laughs for no real reason. Right now, I'm more like a trained mutt in an animal variety show.

Of course, I have no idea what would happen to the world if Haruhi became aware of all these phenomena.

By the way, there were only two people involved in that beginning conversation that just happened, here on the day of the second "SOS Brigade Wanders Around Town" (Temporary Name) in the café in front of the station. After having shamelessly verified that Haruhi would be paying, I calmly explained the situation while sipping my strong coffee. Haruhi acted like she didn't believe a word I said. Well, I guess that was to be expected. Anyone who actually believes this stuff has issues.

I didn't go into any specifics. Just gave her a general summary.

Revealing too many details would only make my mind more suspect. Remember, this is coming from someone who was dragged into Nagato's apartment and subjected to a winding, incomprehensible freak spiel of galactic proportions. I know what I'm talking about.

"That's enough of your lame, dumb jokes."

After Haruhi finished sucking the yellow-green vegetable juice through her straw, she spoke. "Let's get going, then. We can't split up today, so the two of us will have to search every nook and cranny. And I forgot my wallet, so here's the check."

As I stared at the slip of paper reading *830 yen* and tried to formulate an objection, Haruhi gulped down the rest of my coffee, glared at me as if to ensure that she wouldn't hear any complaints, stomped out through the automatic door of the café, and stood outside with her arms crossed.

That was half a year ago. Now that I stop and think about it, the past six months have been filled with strange happenings. The SOS Brigade is still officially named the "**S**ave the world by **O**verloading it with fun Haruhi **S**uzumiya Brigade," which makes me shiver, and I still have no idea where or how this brigade has overloaded the world with fun. Besides, the only one who ever gets psyched up about anything is Haruhi. The purpose and activities of this brigade remain, as always, a mystery. Apparently, her goal is to have fun with aliens, kidnap time travelers, and battle alongside espers. As of this point, Haruhi believes that she has yet to succeed.

That would be because Haruhi thinks that she hasn't met aliens, time travelers, and espers. Since she didn't believe me when I was kind enough to tell her the truth about the identities of the three other people in the SOS Brigade, it's no longer my concern.

And so the SOS Brigade has yet to achieve its goal, and consequently has yet to lose its purpose and happily disband. Which is why to this day, this organization unrecognized by the school continues to exist in a corner of the clubhouse.

Naturally, the five members, including me, are still parasites in the literary club room. The student council executive committee has apparently chosen to ignore the SOS Brigade in every possible way. While they brushed aside my charter application, they didn't say a word about our illegal takeover of the club room. Maybe because Yuki Nagato, who was originally the only literary club member, hasn't said a word. I would deduce that they have determined that feigning ignorance would be much healthier than talking to Haruhi.

Nobody would step on a mine that has *this will explode if you step on it* spelled out in every language in neon lights. I know I wouldn't. If I had known back when I entered this school, I wouldn't have talked to that sour-faced girl sitting behind me in class.

An ordinary high school student who accidentally tripped a bomb and is now currently running in circles like an idiot while holding down the trigger. That would be my current position. And this bomb labeled *Haruhi Suzumiya* doesn't have a timer counting down the time left to when it'll explode. We don't know when it'll explode, how much damage it will cause, what's inside, or if it's even a bomb. It might be just some piece of junk someone said was a bomb. Can't even be sure about that.

I can't seem to find the garbage chute for dangerous items, which means that this personally dangerous thing is practically cemented to my hand.

Seriously, how am I supposed to get rid of this girl?

CHAPTER 1

Schoolwide events are an indispensable part of school, though they happen sporadically. Which reminds me, my high school had an athletic festival last month. I was pretty skeptical when Haruhi mentioned having the SOS Brigade participate in the exhibition relay during the interclub meet, but what do you know, the SOS Brigade really did participate in a relay. I sure didn't expect to blow away the track team and stomp all over the rugby team, with Haruhi running anchor, crossing the finish line approximately thirteen lengths ahead of the closest runner. As a result, our (excluding me) peculiarity had gone from being whispered about by students to the point where it was buzzing around school like someone had just pulled the fire alarm during class, giving me a headache. Most of the blame lies with Haruhi for coming up with the idea, but the second runner, Nagato, is also at fault. I certainly would never have expected her to run so fast that she might as well have been teleporting. Let me know beforehand, Nagato.

When I asked Nagato what kind of magic she had used, the humorless, alien-made organic android gave me an explanation using terms like "energy level" and "quantum leap," which I appreciated, but seeing as how I had already given up on a career in the sciences and had chosen the path of liberal arts, I had no idea what she was talking about. Not that I wanted to know.

Once the crazy athletic festival was over, I eagerly anticipated the coming of a new month, only to learn that we had a cultural festival coming up. At this very moment, our lame prefectural high school was preparing for the event. Except that the only ones preparing were the teachers, executive committee members, and the members of any cultural clubs, for which this was their one opportunity to shine.

Of course, a club must be recognized before it can hold any club activities, and since the SOS Brigade had yet to be recognized, we had no need to engage in any creative preparations. Though I wouldn't have minded picking up some stray cat in the neighborhood and throwing it into a cage with a sign saying *extraterrestrial beast* as some sort of exhibition. But the people who didn't get the joke would probably make a fuss, and the ones who did get it would only ridicule us. Besides, there was no reason for me to stretch my mind to come up with something for the festival. I had no motivation to do it. A cultural festival at a typical high school like ours will always be dull. If you don't believe me, go take a peek at any school that's having a festival. You will then learn the reality that it's just another school event.

By the way, if you're wondering what 1-5, the class Haruhi and I are in, is doing, we copped out and went with some random survey. After Asakura ran off somewhere last spring, no other student in this class was crazy enough to take up the leadership position. The current plan only came after homeroom teacher Okabe strained to come up with an idea during an extended and uncomfortable homeroom period. Nobody was for or against it, so the matter was settled when class ended and we ran out of time. Nobody even knew what the survey would be about. Or who would have fun doing this. Though I doubt anyone would ever enjoy it. But that's how it goes. Work hard, people.

And with that, feeling completely languid, I performed my daily ritual of heading to the club room. Why? Because the girl stomping next to me was saying the following.

"A survey is so dumb."

She made a face like she'd accidentally poured sauce on her natto.

"Where's the fun in that? I totally don't get it!"

"Then you should have spoken up. Didn't you see how Okabe looked like we were holding a wake in the classroom?"

"Doesn't matter. I have no intention of participating in anything the class does. There's no fun in doing anything with those people."

"Except I vaguely remember you contributing to the class winning the all-around championship. Weren't you the one who ran anchor and won the short, medium, and long medley relays? Or was that someone else?"

"That's different."

"How is it different?"

"This is a cultural festival. Or you could call it a campus festival. Though I suppose you wouldn't use the word 'campus' when talking about a public school. Whatever. The cultural festival is the super most important event of the year, right?"

"Really?"

"Really!" she said as she nodded fervently. And then she announced. To me. The following proclamation:

"We, the SOS Brigade, will be doing something much more fun!"

As Haruhi Suzumiya spoke, her face was shining with resolve, like Hannibal deciding to cross the Alps during the Second Punic War.

Only on the surface, though.

Not a single time during the past six months has Haruhi's "something fun" led to anything remotely pleasant for me. Almost all cases end with exhaustion. At least, Asahina and I end up exhausted, but we're the only normal human beings here. As far as I can tell, it's common knowledge on this planet that Haruhi is not a normal person. And I seriously doubt that Koizumi's disposition can be considered normal human behavior. And Nagato isn't even human.

Now that I've gotten involved with this bunch, how am I supposed to get through high school living like a complete stranger to myself? I really don't want to repeat what I had to do six months ago. Never want to do something that rash again. Just thinking about it — someone give me a gun — makes me want to shoot myself in the head. I'd like to extract and burn the brain cells containing the memories of that incident. I don't know how Haruhi felt about it, though.

Since I was busy with devising a way to erase those memories, I didn't hear what the squawking girl next to me said.

"Hey, Kyon. Are you listening?"

"No, not really. What about it?"

"The cultural festival, the cultural festival. You should be a bit more excited. You can only experience the cultural festival as a first-year high school student once."

"Well, yeah. No reason to make a fuss about it, though."

"Yes, there is. Festivals don't happen very often. It wouldn't be a festival if people didn't go wild. That's what happens at all the school festivals I heard of."

"Your middle school really went overboard, huh?"

"Totally not. It wasn't the least bit fun. That's why this high school cultural festival has to be more fun."

"What would you consider fun then?"

"Real ghosts in a haunted house, stairs where the number of steps suddenly increase, the Seven Wonders of the World turn into the Thirteen Wonders, the principal's hair tripling in size into an Afro, the school building transforms and fights with some monster that comes out of the ocean, or 'plum' becoming a seasonal word for 'fall.' That kind of stuff."

Now, I stopped listening halfway, so I missed everything after the stairs part. Maybe someone who has the time could give me a rundown.

". . . well, fine. I'll give you a thorough explanation once we get to the club room."

Haruhi apparently lost her good mood and fell into a sullen silence. We marched on, reaching the club room door in no time. Underneath the plate reading *Literary Club* was a scrap of paper with the words *with the SOS Brigade* scribbled on it. "We've been here for half a year. Nobody can say that this room isn't ours." And with that, she began arbitrarily asserting her occupational rights and started replacing the plate itself before I could stop her. People need to know when to be discreet.

Haruhi opened the door without knocking, and I was able to see a fairy standing in the club room. Her eyes met mine, and her face lit up with a smile like the personification of a lily flower.

"Ah . . . hello."

Sweeping the room with a broom, dressed in a maid outfit, was the SOS Brigade's tea-brewing pride and joy, Mikuru Asahina. As always, she welcomed me with a smile as though she were a fairy living in this club room. Maybe she really is a fairy or something like that. That seems more appropriate than saying she's a time traveler.

Back when the brigade was established, Haruhi gave the incomprehensible reason of "I was thinking that we need a mascot character" when she dragged Asahina here. And then Haruhi forced her into a maid outfit, and ever since, she does a complete transformation into the SOS Brigade maid after school every day. Not because she has a few screws loose in her head, but because she's such a sweet girl that it brings tears to my eyes.

Asahina has dressed up as a bunny girl, nurse, and cheerleader, but I have to say that she looks best as a maid. As for why, this outfit, while serving no purpose, avoids being suggestive in any way, and I'd rather it stay that way. And I might as well take this opportunity to inform everyone that the majority of Haruhi's actions serve no purpose.

But they often lead to something else happening, and that something else usually ends up making trouble for the rest of us. I wish everything she did was meaningless.

One of the few good things Haruhi has done — actually, the only good thing she's done — is creating this maid version of Asahina. She looks so good it makes me light-headed. This is the only time I can't fault one of Haruhi's ideas. I don't know where she got the costume or how much it cost, but Haruhi has pretty good fashion sense. Of course, Asahina would look like a supermodel no matter what she was wearing.

"I'll have tea ready at once," Asahina murmured in her cute voice as she placed the broom in the closet. She then ran over to the cupboard and began taking out our individual cups.

I felt something hard drive into my side. Apparently, Haruhi had elbowed me.

"You're squinting."

Apparently, my eyes naturally squint when appreciating Asahina's loveliness. Anybody else would do the same if they were in the presence of the adorable, graceful, and bashful Asahina.

Haruhi took the armband labeled *Chief* off the desk where the pyramid labeled *Chief* was resting, and put it on. She then plopped into a metal chair and leaned back, glaring around the room.

The other brigade member in the room was sitting at the corner of the table reading a thick book.

"..."

Staring at the pages without looking up even once was the first-year literary club member who was, as far as Haruhi was concerned, like "a bonus that came with the room after taking it over"— Yuki Nagato.

The classmate who stands out as much as nitrogen in the Earth's atmosphere has the strangest profile out of all of us. You could say that her background is even more eccentric than Haruhi's. Haruhi's makes absolutely no sense at all, but Nagato's kind of makes sense — which just confuses me more. If I believe what Nagato says, then this silent-expressionless-emotionless-heartless-quadruple-combo short-haired petite female student isn't human but an alien-made communication machine. Don't ask me what that is. I don't know. She said so herself, so I have nothing to add. Apparently, it's true. But it's a secret Haruhi doesn't know about. Haruhi just thinks that she's "a slightly odd bookworm" and nothing else.

Though from an objective standpoint, I'm thinking "slightly" is a bit off.

"Where's Koizumi?"

Haruhi's sharp glare shot to Asahina. Asahina unconsciously flinched.

"I-I don't know. He hasn't showed up yet. He sure is late. . . ."

She carefully took tea leaves from the tea caddy and placed them into the teapot. I casually surveyed the garment rack in the corner of the room. It contained a number of outfits, as though this were a dressing room for the drama club. From left to right, nurse outfit, bunny, summer maid, cheerleader, yukata, doctor's coat, leopard skin, frog costume, some fluttery transparent thing I didn't recognize, et cetera, et cetera.

Each and every one of them has been graced by the warmth of Asahina's skin over the past six months. There was no meaning in Asahina wearing any of these. It was solely for the sake of satisfying Haruhi. Maybe she had some kind of trauma from her childhood. Like her parents wouldn't buy her a Barbie doll. Which was why she was playing with Asahina now. Consequently, Asahina's trauma built steadily, and my eyes were treated to a divine feast. Well, if you add it all up, I guess more people ended up happy than not, so I just kept my mouth shut.

"Mikuru, tea."

"Y-yes. Right away."

Asahina hurriedly poured green tea into the teacup labeled *Haruhi* in Magic Marker before placing it on a tray and slowly carrying it over.

Haruhi blew on the hot tea before speaking like a master of flower arranging criticizing the ineptitude of an apprentice.

"Mikuru, I'm pretty sure I've told you this before. Do you remember?"

"What?"

Asahina clung to the tray nervously.

"What was it again?" She tilted her head questioningly like a java sparrow trying to remember the taste of the hemp seeds it ate the day before.

Haruhi set her teacup on the desk. "When you carry the tea over, you're supposed to trip and spill the tea once every three times! You're not acting the least bit like a clumsy maid!"

"Wha — Ah . . . I'm sorry."

Asahina shrugged. This was the first I'd heard of such an order. So what, Haruhi thinks that all maids are clumsy?

"That's fine, Mikuru. You can practice on Kyon. Make sure the teacup ends up flipped over on his head."

"Huh?"

That was Asahina's response as she turned and glanced at me. I was looking around for a drill so I could plug up that empty hole in Haruhi's head, but unfortunately I couldn't find one, so instead I just sat and sighed.

"Asahina, only people with mental issues find Haruhi's jokes funny."

You should have learned that by now. But I refrained from voicing that last sentiment.

Haruhi's eyes narrowed.

"Hey, stupid. I'm not joking! I'm always serious!"

Then it must be worse than we thought. You should go get a CT scan. And if I get really pissed whenever you call me stupid, does that mean I lack a sense of humor?

"Fine. I'll show you how it's done. You go next, Mikuru."

Haruhi leapt from her metal chair, swiped the tray from the babbling Asahina, picked up the teapot, and began pouring tea into the cup marked with my name.

As I watched in a daze, Haruhi set the teacup on the tray, spilling a considerable amount. She verified my location before nodding and heading toward my position, which was when I plucked the teacup from the side.

"Hey! Don't interfere!"

Interfere? If someone's willing to stand still while hot tea is being poured onto his head, he's either one hell of a nice guy or some kind of insurance scam artist.

I remained standing as I drank the green tea Haruhi had poured and pondered why it tasted so different from Asahina's tea when they used the same tea leaves. That was a no-brainer. The difference would be in the spice called love. If Asahina were

a wild white rose in bloom, then this girl would be some kind of special rose that was all thorns and never bloomed. And bore no fruit, naturally.

Haruhi glared at me with chastising eyes as I silently drank my tea.

"Hmph."

With a flip of her hair, she returned to the chief's desk. Slurp. She made a face like she was drinking boiling, bitter medicine.

Asahina, relieved, returned to her service, pouring tea into Nagato's cup and placing it in front of the reading girl.

Nagato didn't even flinch. She remained fixed on her hardcover. You should have at least showed a little gratitude. It'd probably take Taniguchi three days to finish savoring that tea.

". . ."

Nagato continued flipping through the pages without looking up. Since that was how it always was, Asahina didn't actually mind and went to put her own teacup on standby.

That was when the fifth brigade member walked in, despite the fact that no one would have cared if he never showed up.

"Terribly sorry I'm late. Homeroom lasted longer than usual."

The one who opened the door with a seemingly harmless smile beaming on his face would be, according to Haruhi, the mysterious transfer student, Itsuki Koizumi. With a smile like that on his face, I would never introduce him, as a friend, to my girlfriend. That is, if I had one.

"It appears I'm the last one. I apologize if I delayed the meeting. Or should I treat everyone to something?"

"Meeting? What's that? I didn't hear anything about a meeting."

"I forgot to tell you," Haruhi said as she rested her chin in her hands. "I told everyone else during lunch. Just figured I could tell you whenever."

"How can you have time to go to other classrooms yet not find time to tell the person sitting in front of you in your own classroom?"

"Who cares? It's all the same anyway. The issue isn't what you heard or when you heard it, but what you're doing right now."

Her words may sound impressive on the surface, but it has been well established that anything she does only serves to worsen my mood.

"Moving on, time to think about what to do now!"

Do a better job of distinguishing between now as in this very instant or now as in the near future. And would the subject of that sentence be a singular I or a plural we?

"Of course, I mean all of us. This will be an SOS Brigade event."

"Event?" I asked.

"Weren't you listening? The only event this time of year is the cultural festival!"

"That isn't a brigade event. It is a school event. If you wanted to promote the cultural festival so badly, you should have run in the elections for the executive committee. You'd be flooded with pointless menial tasks to do."

"That would defeat the purpose. We need to create an SOS Brigade–style activity. I've spent too much effort building up this brigade! Not a soul in this school should be able to say that they don't know about this super-hot group," Haruhi said.

What would constitute an SOS Brigade–style activity? I thought back on the SOS Brigade activities over the past six months and became a bit depressed.

You have it easy since you just throw out whatever idea comes to your mind, but what about the suffering Asahina and I have to go through? Koizumi just smiles shrewdly and Nagato is absolutely no help when it comes to brainstorming. Ah, I guess

Asahina isn't exactly normal, but she's cute, so that makes it all okay. She just needs to stand there as a treat for my eyes and a balm for my weary soul.

"We have to meet their expectations," Haruhi said with a contemplative look on her face.

Who exactly is expecting anything from the SOS Brigade? That's worth having a survey about. And I don't see how you've built up this brigade when our standing is still below that of a student association and our number of members hasn't increased. Since more members would only complicate the situation, I can live without them, but the way things look now, this derailed Haruhi express is going to keep skidding on. And the only passengers are the five of us. I'd like to find a scapegoat to take my place. I'll even pay an hourly wage. I'm willing to give a hundred yen per.

Haruhi drained her first cup in thirty seconds and requested a second from Asahina.

"What about you, Mikuru? What are you guys doing?"

"Um . . . you mean my class? A yakisoba café . . ."

"You're probably a waitress, right?"

Asahina's eyes widened.

"How did you know? I wanted to cook, but everyone told me to be a waitress . . ."

Haruhi had a contemplative look on her face again. Based on experience, that look in her eyes meant she couldn't be thinking about anything good. And those eyes were glancing toward the garment rack. The expression on her face suggested she had just realized that she had yet to put Asahina in a waitress outfit.

Now Haruhi had a brooding look on her face.

"What about your class, Koizumi?"

Koizumi shrugged slightly. "We've decided to do a play, but the class is divided between doing an original work and a classical piece. The cultural festival is fast approaching yet they are still debating. It's a fierce argument, so some time will be needed before a conclusion can be reached."

How lucky of you to be in such a lively class. Sounds like a pain, though.

"Hmm."

Haruhi's floating gaze drifted to the remaining member, who had yet to speak a word.

"Yuki?"

The book-loving pseudo-alien looked up like a prairie dog sensing rain.

"Fortune-telling," she responded in her usual flat voice.

"Fortune-telling?" I unconsciously echoed.

"Yes."

Nagato nodded with a face devoid of expression, like she wasn't even breathing.

"You're telling fortunes?

"Yes."

Nagato telling fortunes? Sure you don't mean telling the future? I pictured Nagato in black pointy hat and robe and holding out a crystal ball before a couple and saying, "You will break up in fifty-eight days, three hours, and five minutes," with a straight face. You could lie, you know.

Then again, I don't actually know if Nagato can see the future.

"So Asahina's class is running a refreshment booth, Koizumi's is doing a play, and Nagato's is holding a fortune-telling convention. They all sound infinitely more fun than the listless survey our class is doing. Yeah, how's this? Let's combine everything and do a fortune-telling survey play café," I suggested.

"Stop sounding like an idiot. Let's get this meeting started."

Haruhi instantly rejected my valuable opinion and walked over to the whiteboard. She tapped the board with a long antenna-like pointer.

"There's nothing written on it. What am I supposed to be looking at?"

"There will be soon. Mikuru, you're the secretary, so take down every word I say."

I had no idea when Asahina became the secretary. I doubted anyone did. Apparently, Haruhi just decided that a moment ago.

Asahina, tea girl and now secretary, held a felt-tip pen, stood next to the whiteboard, and looked up at Haruhi's face next to her.

And then Haruhi suddenly spoke in a triumphant voice.

"We, the SOS Brigade, will be screening a movie!"

I really don't know what kind of mutation is going on inside of Haruhi's head. I'll just not think about it. It's nothing new. Still, this isn't a meeting. It's just you delivering a speech on general policy, isn't it?

"..."

"That's how it always is," Koizumi whispered to me.

The elegant smile he had made me want to draw on his face. His graceful lips remained curved up.

"Suzumiya had decided what we were going to do from the very beginning. That doesn't leave any room for discussion. Now then, did you say something you shouldn't have again?"

Pretty sure I didn't say anything remotely related to movies today. Maybe she saw a low-budget C-movie late last night and its crappiness put her in a miserable mood?

"There's something I've always wondered about," Haruhi continued cheerfully, convinced that her speech had touched every member in the audience.

"..."

I'm wondering about what exactly is inside your head.

"You often see people die in the last episode of TV shows and the like. Doesn't that feel really unnatural? Why do they just happen to die at that time? It's strange. That's why I hate anything where someone dies at the end. I would never make a movie like that!"

"Are you talking about movies or TV shows?"

"I said that we're going to screen a movie, didn't I? Even those old earthen statues from the Tumulus period had better ears than you. Imprint every word I say into your memory with no mistakes."

If I'm gonna bother memorizing your insane babbling, it'd be much more productive to memorize every last station on the rail line that runs nearby.

Asahina wrote *movie screening* in round letters that really didn't look like the handwriting of a former calligraphy club member. Haruhi took a glance before nodding, satisfied.

"There you have it. We're all under agreement then?"

She sounded as cheerful as a weather forecaster verifying the end of the rainy season.

"What do you even mean?" I asked.

A natural response. All I know is that we're screening a movie. Who's going to hook us up with a film? Does she have an acquaintance at Buena Vista International or something?

But Haruhi's eyes continued to shine with reckless abandon.

"Kyon, you're not too bright. We're going to make a movie. And then we'll screen it at the cultural festival. With *Presented by the SOS Brigade* in the credits!"

"When did we turn into the film society?"

"What are you talking about? This will absolutely be the SOS Brigade. I don't remember turning into a stupid film society."

If the film society people were to hear those words, they'd probably be pissed.

"It's already been decided. Double jeopardy! Plea bargaining will be ignored!"

If the SOS Brigade jury foreman says so, then I guess the verdict won't be overturned. Who the hell put Haruhi in the leadership position . . . or now that I think about it, she put herself in that position. Looks like loud and eager people are the ones who become important no matter what world you're in. Consequently, good Samaritans who tend to go with the flow like Asahina and me end up being abused. That's just one of the contradictions in the reality of this cruel and heartless world.

I pondered the profound subject of what could be considered an ideal society.

"I see."

Koizumi interrupted like he had just figured something out. He smiled at both Haruhi and me.

"I understand perfectly."

Hey, Koizumi. Don't just accept the bomb Haruhi dropped on us. Don't you have your own opinion on this?

Koizumi gently flipped the forelocks of his hair.

"In other words, we're going to make an independent film, gather an audience, and screen the movie. Am I correct?"

"You are correct!"

Haruhi continued tapping the board with her antenna, and Asahina's shoulders flinched. Regardless, Asahina mustered the courage to voice her question.

"But . . . why did you decide to make a movie?"

"Last night, I was having trouble getting to sleep."

Haruhi waved the antenna in front of her face like a windshield wiper.

"So I turned on the TV, and there was this weird movie on.

Didn't really want to watch it, but I didn't have anything else to do, so I did."

Figured as much.

"And it was such a horrible movie, so bad I wanted to make an international prank call to the director's house. So then I thought"— she stuck the tip of the pointer at Asahina's petite face as she continued —"if this is the best they can do, I can make a movie that's much better!"

". . ."

Haruhi puffed up her chest, full of confidence.

"So I figured that it was worth a shot. You have a problem with that?"

Asahina furiously shook her head like she was terrified. Even if she did have a complaint, she would never voice it. Koizumi was just a yes-man. Nagato never said anything to begin with, which meant it was inevitable for me to speak up.

"I don't care if you're aiming to be a movie director or to be a producer. You can do whatever you want with your life. And so the rest of us can do whatever we wish and want, right?"

"What are you talking about?" Haruhi puckered her lips like a duck's bill.

I patiently explained to her, "You say you want to make a movie. We haven't said anything yet. If we say we don't want to, what would you do? A director isn't enough to make a movie."

"Don't worry. I've got most of the script thought through."

"No, what I'm trying to say is that —"

"There's nothing for you to fret about. Just follow me like always. No need to worry."

I'm worried.

"Leave the planning to me. I'll take care of everything."

Now I'm even more worried.

"You sure complain a lot. I said we're gonna do it, which means we're gonna do it. Our goal is to place first in the cultural festival's best-event poll! Then that unreasonable student council may even recognize the SOS Brigade as a club — no! I'll definitely make them recognize us. Which means that first, we need public opinion on our side!"

Public opinion and poll results aren't necessarily correlated.

I attempted to put up resistance.

"What about production costs?"

"We have a budget."

Where? I can't see the student council giving a budget to this brigade, which moves rather openly for an underground organization.

"We have the literary club's cut."

"That would be the literary club's budget. It's not for you to use."

"But Yuki said it was fine."

Good grief. I looked at Nagato's face. She deliberately looked up at me without saying a word before returning to her book.

You sure nobody wants to join the literary club? Not that I'm gonna ask, but I wouldn't be surprised if Nagato had driven this club to the verge of being cut. Apparently, she knew beforehand that Haruhi would be showing up. I sure feel sorry for anyone who had their heart set on joining the literary club. If you're out there, do work hard to reclaim what was originally the literary club back from Haruhi.

Haruhi, oblivious to my inner monologue, waved her antenna around.

"Everyone got that? This takes priority over whatever your class is doing! If you have any objections, tell me after the festival. Got it? The director's orders are absolute!" Haruhi shouted, completely unaware of what was going on around her, like a polar bear in the zoo who had just been given an ice cube in the middle of summer.

From brigade chief to director? What's she planning on being in the end? Please don't say God.

"Then that's all for today! I have to do some thinking about casting and sponsors. The producer has lots of work to do!"

I'm not really sure what the producer does, but in any case, what is she planning on doing? Sponsors?

Slam.

A dull sound rang through the air. I turned to find that Nagato had closed her book. That sound had become the signal for the SOS Brigade to pack up and go home for the day.

After saying that she would go into details tomorrow, Haruhi shot off like a cat hearing a tin can being opened. Not that I really wanted to hear any further details.

"Splendid, don't you think?"

That obviously came from Koizumi.

"I'm quite relieved that we aren't trying to capture an extraterrestrial beast to put in a freak show or shooting down a UFO to exhibit its interior."

I felt like I'd heard this before.

The smiling esper chuckled with his mouth closed.

"Besides, I am interested in finding out what kind of movie Suzumiya intends to make. Though I can probably guess what she has in mind."

Koizumi gave Asahina, putting away the teacups, a sidelong glance.

"It would appear that this will be a fun cultural festival. Quite fascinating."

I also turned to look at Asahina. I watched as her hair band bounced up and down.

"Ah. Wh-what is it?"

Asahina realized that we two rascals were staring at her and stopped what she was doing as her cheeks flamed.

I murmured in my heart.

No, it's nothing. Just thinking about what costume Haruhi will bring next. That's all.

Once she was done getting ready to go home — well, it just meant putting her book in her bag — Nagato silently stood and silently walked out the open door. Maybe she was reading a book about fortune-telling. It was a foreign book, so I wouldn't know.

"But, yeah," I muttered.

A movie . . . A movie, huh.

To be honest, I was somewhat interested. Not as interested as Koizumi, though. My interest was only at the continental-shelf level, not ocean-floor levels.

I suppose I could at least look forward to it.

Since I'm guessing nobody's expecting much.

And I was already eating my words. I shouldn't have bothered looking forward to this.

It was after school the next day. I had an extremely unhappy look on my face.

Presented by: SOS Brigade
Executive Supervisor/Executive Director/
Direction/Scenario: Haruhi Suzumiya
Lead Actress: Mikuru Asahina
Lead Actor: Itsuki Koizumi
Supporting Actress: Yuki Nagato

Assistant Director/Cameraman/Editing/
Carrying Things/Maid/Errand Boy/Roundsman/
Other Menial Tasks: Kyon

Only one thing crossed my mind after I saw what was written on the scrap of paper.

"So? What's my role?"

"Exactly what it says on there." Haruhi waved the pointer like a conductor. "You're backstage staff. The cast is as written. Perfect casting, don't you think?"

". . ."

"I'm the lead character?" Asahina asked in a small voice. She was dressed in her uniform instead of the maid outfit. Haruhi had told her she didn't have to wear it. It looked like Haruhi was planning on taking her somewhere.

"Um, I'd rather not be in a conspicuous role . . ." Asahina appealed to Haruhi with a distressed look on her face.

". . ."

"No," Haruhi replied. "You need to stand out, Mikuru. You're like the trademark of this brigade. You should start to practice signing autographs. There will probably be a lot of requests from the audience at the premiere."

Premiere? Where are you going to have that?

Asahina sounded quite nervous.

". . . But I can't act."

"Don't worry. I'll coach you through it perfectly."

Asahina looked up at me fearfully and sadly lowered her eyelashes.

We were the only three people in the room. Nagato and Koizumi were late because of meetings about what their classes are doing. I didn't see how it could require staying after school. They could just do something random. Guess a lot more classes are serious about this stuff than I thought.

"Anyway, Yuki and Koizumi aren't very dependable," Haruhi said before turning her directionless indignation toward me. "I told them that this should take priority yet they're late because of class activities. I'll need to give them a strong warning."

It's just that Nagato and Koizumi actually feel a sense of belonging to their class. The three of us are the strange ones for being in this place at this time of year.

I suddenly thought of something.

"Asahina, don't you need to participate in your class meeting?"

"Mmm, I'm just a waitress, so the only thing left for me to do would be a costume fitting. I wonder what they'll have us wear. I'm kind of looking forward to it." Asahina smiled with a faint flush in her cheeks.

It would appear that she's grown completely accustomed to dressing up in costumes. I guess wearing a costume that's appropriate for the situation beats wearing a meaningless costume for SOS Brigade purposes. There's nothing strange about a waitress in a yakisoba café. Makes a lot more sense than a maid in the literary club room.

But Haruhi apparently blew her response way out of proportion.

"What's that, Mikuru? You were dying to be a waitress? You should have told me sooner! That's easy enough. I'll get an outfit for you."

I suppose I shouldn't talk like this has nothing to do with me, but club members in a club room who aren't wearing a uniform just look out of place. The nurse outfit was pretty out there. Might as well stick with the maid outfit then . . . or I guess that's just personal preference.

"Well, that's fine."

Haruhi turned back to me. "Kyon, do you know what the most important thing required to make a movie is?"

Well, now. I scanned through all the movies that had left a deep impression on me. After some consideration, I confidently delivered my answer.

"Innovative concepts and earnest passion in the production, right?"

"It's nothing abstract like that." Haruhi denied me. "It's the camera, obviously. How do you film a movie without equipment?"

I suppose, but I wasn't trying to be utilitarian. . . . Whatever. I'm not so fervent about innovative concepts or earnest passion or knowledgeable enough about film theory to put up an argument.

"There you have it then." Haruhi retracted the pointer and tossed it on the chief's desk. "We're going to go scrounge up a video camera now."

I heard a chair clang next to me. I looked up to see that Asahina's face had turned pale. I suppose that was to be expected. The computer currently enshrined in this club room was swiped from the computer society through Haruhi's coercive con scheme. And during that incident, Asahina had been the sacrifice.

Strands of Asahina's chestnut hair trembled. Her lips, like a pink shell, quivered.

"U-u-u-um, Su-Suzumiya. That's right. I need to go back to the classroom right away to take care of something."

"Shut up."

A terrifying look on Haruhi's face. Asahina, half out of her chair, gave a soft squeal before sinking back into her chair.

Haruhi suddenly grinned. "Don't worry."

There isn't a single precedent of you telling us not to worry where we actually didn't need to worry.

"I won't be using Mikuru's body as payment this time. I just need your help for a bit."

Asahina looked at me like a calf about to be loaded onto a truck. I refrained from bursting into a chorus of "Dona Dona" and turned to Haruhi.

"Tell us what we're helping you with. Or else Asahina and I aren't budging a step."

Haruhi's face plainly said that she had no idea what we were so concerned about. "We're going to go round up sponsors. We'll make a better impression if the lead actress is along, right? You're also coming. You can carry stuff for us."

CHAPTER 2

It was supposed to be fall already, but the temperature had yet to cool. I guess Earth finally went senile and forgot to change the season in Japan to fall. The summer heat appeared set to continue diligently into extra innings with no end in sight. It would stick around forever unless someone hit a walk-off home run. Though I got the feeling that by that point, fall would be long gone and we'd be into winter.

Haruhi told us that it might take a while, so we grabbed our book bags as we left school. I wondered where Haruhi was headed as she rapidly descended the hill. I really doubt we can find a sponsor willing to donate money for a high school original movie. Maybe if we were a research society, but we're an absolutely pointless, unexplained group that's existed for over half a year despite the fact that we don't know why we're here. I wouldn't be surprised if nobody even opened their door for us.

After we reached the bottom of the hill, we boarded the local line of the private railway and got off at the third station. We were near the cherry-tree-lined path where Asahina and I had taken a stroll. I saw a huge department store as well as a shopping district. A relatively busy place.

With Asahina and me in her tracks, Haruhi headed straight into the shopping district.

"Here."

The place Haruhi pointed to after she had finally stopped was an electronics store.

"I see," I said. Apparently, she intends to wrangle the equipment for filming the movie out of this place.

How?

"Hold on. I'm going to go negotiate."

Haruhi handed me her bag and walked into the glass-walled store.

Asahina hid behind me, looking fearfully into the store illuminated by the lighting display, like a shy grade-schooler visiting a friend's house for the first time. I was all pumped up to protect Asahina this time, observing Haruhi's back as she waved and then began talking to a middle-aged man who looked to be the manager. If Haruhi even remotely looks like she's about to do anything fishy, I'll take Asahina under my arm and run for it.

On the other side of the glass, Haruhi was talking while pointing to some item on display, then to herself, and then to the guy. And the guy was just nodding. I should probably warn him not to acquiesce so readily.

Eventually, Haruhi spun around and pointed to the two of us, who were standing outside the glass door ready to escape at a moment's notice. She then smiled like she'd eaten some weird 'shrooms and returned to her animated speech.

"I wonder what she's doing. . . . ," Asahina — hiding behind me to the side — said questioningly as she repeatedly stuck her face out for a peek before drawing it back.

If someone from the future doesn't know, there's no way I would.

"Beats me. She's probably telling the guy to give her his most advanced digital handheld video camera free of charge."

She's a girl capable of saying stuff like that with a straight face. One slip and you'll have her thinking that the world revolves around her.

I sighed. "What a pain."

I recall posing a query to Nagato not too long ago.

Haruhi believes her values and judgment to be absolute. And it's certain that she has no idea that other people, actually most people, may think or feel differently. If you want to achieve faster-than-light travel, let Haruhi on your spaceship. She'll just simply ignore the theory of relativity for you.

When I mentioned this to Nagato, the reticent pseudo-alien responded with the following.

"Your belief is most likely correct."

One of Nagato's more meaningful sentences. A joke that wasn't funny. That is the existence of Haruhi Suzumiya.

"Ah, it looks like they're done talking." Asahina's hushed voice brought me out of my flashback.

As expected, Haruhi emerged from the electronics store looking very pleased. She was carrying a small box in her hands. I looked at the product photo next to the large logo of a well-known electronics maker. If I wasn't mistaken, it looked like a video camera.

"What kind of threats did you make? Hand it over or I'll set fire to the place? Boycott the store? Send prank faxes all night? Go into a violent tantrum on the spot? Self-destruct without any warning?"

"Are you retarded? I wouldn't use those kinds of blackmail tactics."

Haruhi was merrily walking under the canopy of the shopping district.

"The first step was a success. Everything's going well."

I walked after her, forced to carry the box containing the video camera, as I watched her straight hair swaying across her back.

"I'm asking how you got such an expensive item for free. Are you holding something over him?"

Yeah, the first thing she said after leaving the store was "Got it." If he's giving away stuff, hook me up. What are the magic words?

Haruhi looked back with a grin on her face. "Nothing special. I said that I wanted to film a movie, so give me a camera, and the guy was like sure and gave it to me. No problem at all."

No problem now maybe, but I have a feeling there will be a problem later on. Or do I just worry too much?

"Stop getting worked up over every little thing. You just need to work enthusiastically as my servant."

Unfortunately, it felt as though last spring, I had accidentally gotten on a ship with the word *Titanic* written across its side. I wanted to send out an SOS at one point, but I regret to say that I don't know Morse code. First of all, I don't have the temperament to just generously be anyone's servant.

"Come on, let's go to the next store!"

Haruhi walked off energetically, arms swinging, amid the crowd of shoppers. I exchanged a look with Asahina before running after Haruhi as she faded into the distance at a pace you'd expect from someone participating in a speed-walking race.

The next place Haruhi visited was a model shop.

Asahina and I were left outside again as Haruhi engaged in negotiations. I was beginning to understand. When Haruhi

pointed at us through the glass, she was actually pointing to Asahina. Like she meant for Asahina to perform some kind of action to serve as payment through services. Asahina, completely oblivious to that fact, was curiously staring at the diorama in the display case. Should I tell her?

After a few minutes of waiting, Haruhi once again emerged from the store carrying a bulky box.

"What is it this time?"

"A weapon," Haruhi replied as she pressed the box on me. Upon a closer look, I saw that the box contained something like a plastic model. And it appeared to be a pistol-type firearm. What was she going to do with this?

"We'll use it in the action scenes. Some gun action. A flashy gunfight is one of the basics of entertainment. I'd like to blow up a few buildings while we're at it. Do you happen to know where they sell dynamite? I wonder if the general store sells it."

How would I know? I can at least tell you that you're not going to find any in convenience stores or on the Internet. You might find some lying around if you go to a quarry . . .

. . . was the next thing I was about to say, but I swallowed those words. Think about who this is. I wouldn't put it past her to go off in the dead of night to steal fuses and TNT gunpowder.

I set the boxes containing the video camera and model gun on the ground and turned to Haruhi. "So? What do we do with all this stuff?"

"Take them home with you for now. Then bring them to the club room tomorrow. It'd be a pain to go back to school at this point."

"Me?"

"You."

Haruhi crossed her arms with a cheery look on her face. A sight rarely seen in the classroom. Her SOS Brigade–only smile. Whenever Haruhi smiled like this, I ended up having to run around cleaning up after each disaster. Was I the opposite of the straw millionaire?

"Um."

Asahina was timidly raising her hand.

"What should I do . . . ?"

"You're fine, Mikuru. You can go home now. We're done for the day."

Asahina blinked her eyes rapidly like a raccoon cub bewitched by a fox spirit, since the only thing she'd done all day was nervously follow Haruhi around with me. She had no idea why Haruhi forced her to come along.

Haruhi looked like she still had enough energy left to do a second round of cardio exercises as she led us to the nearest station. Apparently that took care of the day's Haruhi-related activities. Either her negotiating skills or underhanded talents had yielded a video camera and a small gun. No expense charged. In other words, they were free.

People used to say that there was nothing more frightening than getting something for free. The problem was, Haruhi wasn't the least bit scared. Actually, if something out there is capable of scaring her, please get in touch with me.

The next day, I found myself lugging excess baggage in addition to my book bag up the hill.

"Yo, Kyon. Whatcha carrying there? A present for some good little children?"

That was Taniguchi, running up next to me. A simple-minded, single-celled idiot. An unmistakably ordinary student you could find anywhere. "Ordinary." What a wonderful word. It means so much to me in my current situation. It has the ring of reality to it.

I hesitated for a moment before passing the lighter of the two plastic bags on to Taniguchi.

"What is this? A model gun? I didn't know you had such a dark hobby."

"Not mine. Haruhi's."

And I suppose I should have followed up by saying, *You shouldn't be so quick to label it as a dark hobby.*

"I really can't picture Suzumiya disassembling and cleaning a Glock by herself."

Neither can I. Which means somebody else is going to be disassembling and reassembling this thing. I should mention that when I was a kid, I once attempted to put together a certain mobile suit, which ended with me giving up when I couldn't attach the right shoulder joint.

"Must be rough for you."

Taniguchi didn't sound the least bit like he thought it was rough for me.

"We could search through all ages and places and the only person willing to babysit Suzumiya would be you. I guarantee it. So hook up with her already."

What the hell is he saying? "I have no intention of attaching myself to Haruhi in any feasible way. The one I would want to attach myself to would be Asahina." As would anyone else if given the choice.

Taniguchi cackled like a demon.

"Yeah, that won't do. She's the angel of North High. A resting spot for the hearts of the male students. Unless you want half the school to stuff you into a bag, don't do anything funny. You wouldn't want me to lose my head and stab you in the back, right?"

"Then I'll go with my next choice, Nagato."

"That's also out of the question. She has more secret admirers than you might expect. Why'd she stop wearing glasses? Did she switch to contacts?"

"Beats me. Ask her yourself."

"From what I've heard, she ignores anyone who tries to talk to her. Apparently, Nagato's class believes that if she says a single word that day, something good or bad will definitely happen."

"Don't talk about Nagato like she's a bamboo flower. That kind of fortune-telling died out long ago. And while it's true that she isn't quite normal, she still has some normal qualities — well, I guess not."

"In other words, you and Suzumiya are made for each other. You're the only one capable of talking with her, and it's best to minimize the number of her potential victims. So take care of it. That reminds me. The cultural festival's coming up. What will your club be doing this time?"

"Stop asking me."

I'm not the SOS Brigade public relations guy.

But Taniguchi calmly continued. "If I ask Suzumiya, she'll just feed me some random nonsense. And there's the fear that if I ask at the wrong time, she'll snap. If I ask Yuki Nagato, she won't give me an answer. And Mikuru Asahina is too hard to approach. Talking to that other guy pisses me off for some reason. So I'm asking you."

The bastard uses some twisted logic. "You're making it sound like I'm some kind of nice guy."

"You're not? As far as I'm concerned, you're the kind of nice guy who'd be willing to walk off a cliff with Asahina."

The front gate was within sight. I took the plastic bag back from Taniguchi with a discouraged look on my face.

I didn't know where Haruhi's trail was going to lead us, but I was definitely thinking that I shouldn't expect anything good. Haruhi and I weren't the only ones walking this path. At least three others I knew of were in for the ride. And while two of those were able to take care of themselves, Asahina wasn't safe on her own. She was so hopeless at predicting what was about to happen to her that you would never think she was a time traveler. Well, I guess that works out.

"Which is why," I said, "somebody has to protect her." Yeah. I'm sounding like a main character now. Except the only thing I'm protecting her from would be Haruhi's evil sexual harassment.

On a roll, I continued. "Since I have this chance, I'm going to protect her. I don't care what all the guys in the school have to say. They can go form their own guardian angels group if they want."

Taniguchi once again cackled like one of those wailing-old-man demons. "Don't overdo it. There's at least one new moon every month."

After delivering what sounded like a notice from a phantom killer, he ducked into the front gate.

As I walked through the hallway in front of our classroom with my burden, I came across Haruhi putting her things into her locker.

I followed suit, stuffing the boxes containing the electronics and the plastic model into the steel locker with my seat number.

"Kyon, we're going to be busy." Without even saying good morning, Haruhi slammed her locker shut and turned to me with a smile like Indian summer.

"Same goes for Mikuru, Yuki, and Koizumi. I won't allow any complaining. The movie script is already bubbling in my mind. It's almost ready to burst. All that remains is to put it into action."

"I see," I answered halfheartedly as I entered the classroom.

My desk was second from the back of the room. We'd changed seating arrangements multiple times since the beginning of the first semester, but I had yet to get a seat in the last row. Because Haruhi always ended up sitting behind me. It had gotten to the point where it had become a bit too unnatural to shrug off, but I still believed it to be coincidence. If I don't have faith in coincidence, coincidence is going to lose confidence in itself.

I'm actually a pretty considerate person. Guess anybody hanging around with Haruhi would have to be. Like a defensive midfielder in a soccer match who has to run down loose balls. Since Haruhi would be the super-offensive-minded forward who's way offside the second someone touches the ball. She might even be standing behind the opposing keeper. Passing the ball to her would just result in the referee raising his flag, but since this is Haruhi, she'd just say it was a mistaken call. In fact, she would say with a straight face that the rule itself makes no sense. She might even start arguing that picking up the ball and running into the goal should count as a goal. The suggestion that she take up rugby would go ignored.

The best way to deal with an audacious person on a rampage would be to casually leave the scene like you never heard a thing or give up and do as she says. The other people in our school year were already doing so.

Which was why when Haruhi disappeared from the classroom when sixth period ended and the final homeroom period began, neither homeroom teacher Okabe nor anybody else said a word about the fact that the seat behind me was empty. Did they not notice? Or were they just pretending not to notice? Not like they could do anything about it. Well, everyone knew it was best to just leave her alone.

I headed for the clubhouse with a bad feeling in my gut before coming to a halt in front of the club room, carrying the bags loaded with assorted boxes.

I could hear something. Asahina's helpless voice crying out. Haruhi's obnoxious voice shouting. She was doing it again.

If I'd opened the door just then, I probably would've witnessed a very fine sight. Being a man with common sense, though, I stoically resisted my fantasies and waited patiently.

After five minutes, the weak struggle inside came to a finish. I was sure Haruhi was standing with her hands on her hips and a triumphant look on her face. Based on the reasoning that a rabbit cannot win against an anaconda, I couldn't see Asahina ever winning.

I knocked.

"Come in!"

A boisterous response from Haruhi. As I wondered about the contents of the paper bags I'd seen that morning, I opened the door and entered the room. The first thing I saw was, in fact, Haruhi's triumphant face. However, I was pretty sick of that sight. With fervent ardor, I turned my attention to the person seated in the metal chair in front of Haruhi.

A waitress sat there looking at me with teary eyes.

". . ."

The waitress, hair disheveled, was doing an impression of Nagato being silent. Her head was drooped. Her full chestnut hair had been tied by Haruhi into two pigtails dangling behind her head. Oddly enough, Nagato was nowhere to be seen.

"Well?" Haruhi asked me with a self-satisfied smirk. Why do you look like you had something to do with this? Asahina's adorableness is her own. . . . Then again.

Y'know? I think it looks nice. How does Asahina feel about it? Not that I have any objections. . . . But isn't the skirt a tad too short?

Asahina was as perfect a waitress as one hundred percent fruit juice is pure. Her clenched fists rested on her knees.

You look so peculiarly perfect, like you're dressed in tailor-made clothes. Which was why I spent a good thirty seconds staring in silence at Asahina before jumping when I was tapped on the shoulder.

"Why, hello. I'm terribly sorry about yesterday. We were supposed to do a run-through of the script today, but I had them wrap things up early. I'm finding myself endlessly running around in circles."

Koizumi's handsome, cheery face peered over my shoulder into the club room.

"Oh?" He smiled merrily. "What do we have here?"

Koizumi passed next to me and set his book bag on the table before sitting in one of the metal chairs. "It looks quite splendid on you, Asahina."

"We all know that already. What we don't know is why a waitress is in this dirty little room that is neither a café nor a family restaurant."

"That's because, Kyon," Haruhi said, "Mikuru will be wearing this outfit in the movie."

"A maid won't work?"

"A maid's job is to go to a rich person's mansion and provide personal service. It's different for a waitress. The goal there is to provide assorted services to an unspecified number of customers in a shop on a corner for seven hundred thirty yen an hour."

I'm not sure if that's a good wage or not, but it's not like Asahina is dressing up to serve in a mansion or work some part-time job. Maybe if Haruhi actually paid her.

"Don't sweat the small stuff! It's all about feeling. I like how this feels."

Who cares about you? How does Asahina feel about this?

"Su-Su-Suzumiya . . . This seems a little too small for me. . . ."

Asahina seemed quite concerned. She was incessantly tugging downward on the hem of her miniskirt. But her motions were too tantalizing. You realize that my eyes can't help but be drawn there, right?

"It's just fine. A perfect fit."

I forced myself to look away and focused instead on Haruhi smiling like a colorful flower blooming in the jungle. Haruhi directed her eyes, always looking forward, at me.

"The concept for our film" — she pointed to Asahina, curled up in a fetal position — "is this!"

"This? Are we doing a documentary on the daily life of a girl working in a café?"

"No. There isn't anything fun about taking secret videos of Mikuru's daily life. The only way you could ever get an interesting story out of filming someone's daily life would be if it was about a person living an extremely eccentric life. Filming the daily life of an ordinary high school student would only be for self-satisfaction."

I fail to see how that would satisfy Asahina, and from an objective point of view, I'd think that self-satisfaction would be important in itself. Besides, Asahina's daily life would actually be considered quite eccentric . . . but I'll keep my mouth shut.

"As the director representing the SOS Brigade, I decided to provide quality entertainment. Just you watch. Every single member of the audience will be on their feet in a standing ovation!"

Upon closer look, I noticed that Haruhi's armband had changed from *Chief* to *Director* at some point. She sure was prepared.

As I watched the female director getting excited by herself, the female lead getting depressed, and the male lead standing back smiling enigmatically like a bystander, I was wondering what exactly was going on. Then the door opened without a sound.

"..."

I thought something big had come to make an appearance. Scared for a moment there that they'd come to retrieve me from my rather short life. It almost made me wonder if I hadn't accidentally stepped into the music room from the movie where Salieri goes to Mozart to commission a requiem.

"..."

As she delivered her signature ellipsis, Yuki Nagato entered the room with a paler face than usual. Only her face was visible. Everything else was covered in black.

I wasn't the only one at a loss for words. Haruhi and Asahina were the same. Koizumi's smile had a hint of surprise tacked on like a tax. Nagato was garbed in clothing strange enough to startle Asahina.

Her body was wrapped in a mantle as dark as a blackout. Her head was covered by a wide-brimmed pointy hat of the same color. She looked like a vampire hunter. Or maybe the Grim Reaper.

As we watched, Nagato silently headed to her designated seat in the corner, withdrew her bag and a hardcover book from under her mantle, and set them on the table.

And — completely ignoring our shock — she began reading her book.

Apparently, it was the costume for her class's fortune-telling convention.

That's what I gathered from Nagato's short responses to Haruhi, who was the first one to recover and issue a rapid string of questions. Nagato's class must have had an extremely resourceful and talented stylist to make Nagato wear such a jolly costume.

In any case, if she walked here from her classroom in this monk-like getup, did it mean this was supposed to be Nagato's way of competing with Asahina? She made guessing what Haruhi was thinking look easy.

An unpleasant silence hung over the room. Only Haruhi looked like she was really happy.

"Yuki, now you understand! Yes, that's it!"

Nagato slowly turned to look at Haruhi before returning to her book.

"That costume is perfect for the role I had in mind! Let the people who put you in that know later. I want to wire them a message to show my appreciation."

Don't. If someone were to receive a message of congratulations from Haruhi, that person would probably suspect some kind of catch and end up being scared of his own shadow. You need to take an objective look at how other people view you.

Haruhi looked to be in high spirits as she hummed the Turkish March while opening her bag and withdrawing a stack of photocopy sheets. She quickly passed them out, looking like Kintaro after wrestling down a black bear.

Not having much choice, I turned my eyes to the sheet of paper. The following passage was scribbled across the page:

"COMBAT WAITRESS:
THE ADVENTURES OF MIKURU ASAHINA" (TENTATIVE)

DRAMATIS PERSONAE
MIKURU ASAHINA: COMBAT WAITRESS FROM THE FUTURE
ITSUKI KOIZUMI: BOY ESPER
YUKI NAGATO: EVIL ALIEN
EXTRAS: PASSERSBY

. . . Yeah, that's just. Yeah.

Has her level of intuition transcended mere disbelief? Or did she hit the mark without even trying? I'm starting to wonder if she's just feigning ignorance. What's with her sharp senses that only work at odd intervals?

As I stood stunned, I was brought back to the real world by the sound of chuckling next to me. The only person with that kind of laugh would be Koizumi.

"Well, this is quite . . ."

I envy how you seem to be enjoying yourself.

"What should I say? Just as one would expect? Indeed, the casting seems quite appropriate for Suzumiya. It's wonderful."

Don't smile at me. It creeps me out.

Asahina was reading the sheet of paper clutched in her slender, violently trembling hands.

"Wha . . ."

A soft cry escaped from her mouth. She turned to me with eyes seeking salvation. Except upon a closer look, her eyes seemed very sad, even reproachful. Like a kind, slightly older female relative scolding a young child whose prank had gone too far. . . . Oh. I remembered. That's right. After the incident six months earlier, I'd revealed their true identities to Haruhi.

Gah. Crap. Is this my fault?

I frantically spun to look at Nagato, the human-contact-purpose humanoid interface clad in a black mantle and black hat.

". . ."

She was silently reading her book.

"I see no problems of consequence," Koizumi later asserted optimistically.

I failed to see the humor in this situation.

"While these circumstances may not invite humor, there is no need for pessimism."

"How do you know?"

"For the simple reason that this is merely casting for a movie. Suzumiya does not actually believe that I am a boy esper. I only play the role of a boy esper named Itsuki Koizumi within the fictional context of the movie."

Koizumi sounded like a tutor talking to a pupil with a really bad memory.

"You can say that the Itsuki Koizumi that exists in reality, myself, and this particular Itsuki are entirely different people. Nobody would confuse a character in a movie with the actor playing the role, right? Even if someone out there were to get the two mixed up, that person would not necessarily be Suzumiya."

"That's not very reassuring. There's no guarantee that what you're saying is right."

"If she were for mixing reality and fiction, then our world would have become the stuff of fantasy long ago. As I mentioned before, Suzumiya is still a person who can think rationally."

I know that. But since Haruhi's rational reasoning is half-possessed, I've been dragged into many bizarre incidents. And Haruhi, the key to all of this, doesn't have a clue about what's happening around her.

"For we must not allow her to discover any evidence of what is happening," Koizumi continued calmly. "There may come a time when we have no choice but to reveal the truth. But not now. Fortunately, Asahina's faction and Nagato's faction are of the same opinion. I would prefer that the current situation never change."

So would I. I don't want to watch the world turn into a huge mess. That can't happen until I've beaten the game that comes out next week or I'll have lingering regrets.

Koizumi was still smiling. "You should worry less about the world and be more concerned about your own safety. Nagato and I can probably be replaced, but you have no understudy."

I took care not to let these feelings of frustration affect me and pretended to be engrossed in pressurizing the gun I now had back in my hands.

Haruhi called it a day after assigning Asahina her costume and announcing the cast. Actually, she apparently wanted to drag Asahina around in her waitress outfit and hold a press conference for the upcoming film, but since Asahina was seriously on the verge of tears, I made Haruhi give up on that idea. It's not like this high school has a journalism club, news club, or advertising club to begin with. Once I brought that up, Haruhi's lips pouted into waterfowl status.

"I suppose you're right."

Amazingly enough, she agreed.

"It's better to keep the details under wraps until the very last second. Kyon, that's rather clever of you. We can't have people ripping us off."

This idea isn't exactly at the level of a Hollywood or Hong Kong film. Who would want a storyboard that's still bubbling in your mind?

"So, Kyon, have the gun ready for use within the day. Filming starts tomorrow. You also need to learn how to use the camera. Ah, that's right. You'll need to move the video data from the camera to the computer and do the editing, so pirate the necessary software. Also . . ."

And once Haruhi had finished dumping a load of assignments on me, she left while humming the theme from *The Great Escape.*

Didn't matter if she was in a good mood or a bad mood, she was always causing trouble for other people. Honestly.

Which was why I was currently face-to-face with another guy, Koizumi, struggling to make the model gun shoot BBs with reference to the instruction manual.

Once Asahina finished changing, she left with sagging shoulders. Nagato, still dressed like a witch invited to a Sabbath, went off somewhere without her bag. I guess Nagato had only come to show us her costume. Based on her record, there may have been some kind of significance in that action. Or she was just showing her face in the club room. She's probably doing something in her classroom at this moment. Like practicing fortune-telling with a crystal ball or whatever.

I got the impression that the level of commotion in the school was slightly increasing on a day-to-day basis. Each time I heard the wind ensemble practicing after school, the crappy horns made fewer mistakes. There were also people cutting up veneer and balsa wood in the shadows of the courtyard. And a growing number of people were dressed in odd costumes like Nagato's.

But this was just a festival at a plain old prefectural high school. I expected a cultural festival without anything extreme or out of the ordinary. As far as I could see, maybe half the student body hadn't given up on working hard to make this a fun festival. Incidentally, our class, 1-5, had just given up on having fun, period. The ones who weren't in a cultural club would probably be really bored that day. And here we had two people who could easily represent the go-straight-home-after-school club, Taniguchi and Kunikida.

"Speaking of cultural festivals . . . ," Taniguchi said.

It was lunchtime. These two-bit characters and I were surrounded by box lunches.

"Speaking of cultural festivals?" Kunikida shot back.

Taniguchi had a sickening smirk on his face that couldn't hold a candle to the refined Koizumi smile. "It's a super-event."

"Don't talk like Haruhi."

Taniguchi's smirk was abruptly wiped from his face. "But it's got nothing to do with me. It pisses me off."

"Why?" Kunikida asked.

"The sight of people having fun when I'm not really annoys me. Especially if it's a boy-girl couple. Gives me homicidal urges. What? Got a problem with that?"

I suppose this is what you would call blind rage.

"And what's with our class? A survey? Ha! Bo-ring. It'll probably just involve asking people what their favorite color is, right? Where's the fun in gathering that information?"

Then why didn't you throw out your brilliant idea? That might have prevented Haruhi from mentioning anything about movies.

Taniguchi swallowed a lunch wiener in one gulp. "I never say anything that will give me work to do. Well, I might say something, but I don't want to end up being put in charge of the mess."

Kunikida voiced his agreement as he took a break from cutting his rolled omelet. "The only people who are going to raise their hands and open their mouths in this situation are those who are easily influenced or have a strong sense of responsibility. If only Asakura were still here."

He threw out the name of our former classmate who had moved to Canada. I break into a cold sweat every time I hear her name. Nagato may have been the one who erased Asakura, but I was the reason it happened. Of course, if Nagato hadn't done anything, I would have been erased, so there isn't any point in feeling bad about it.

"Yeah, that was a waste," Taniguchi said. "Just had to be my A-plus who transferred. I'm really down on my luck. She was the only good thing about being in this class. Damn. Wonder if they'll let me change classes at this point."

"Which class would you want?" Kunikida asked. "Nagato's class? Oh, speaking of which, I saw her walking around in some kind of wizard getup yesterday. What's up with that?"

Beats me. I sure don't know.

"Nagato, huh . . ." Taniguchi turned to me with a look on his face like he'd just found out about a pop quiz in math. He sounded like he had just remembered something.

"When was that again? That time the two of you were all tangled up in the classroom. That was probably just something scripted by Suzumiya. Probably some kind of scheme to surprise me, right? Ain't happening."

I was feeling rather relieved that he'd arbitrarily misunderstood the whole affair . . . Wait, didn't you come back to the classroom to get something you'd forgotten? How could we have possibly known that you would show up — but naturally, I didn't voice this sentiment. Taniguchi was an idiot. Telling an idiot he was an idiot served no purpose. Good thing he was an idiot. I should be thankful.

"At any rate, this sure is boring," Taniguchi lamented while Kunikida concentrated on his box lunch. I looked behind me. Haruhi's desk was empty. Well now. I wondered where Haruhi was marching at that moment.

"I was looking for a good filming location around school," Haruhi told me. "But I totally couldn't find one. I suppose we won't be able to shoot it around here after all. Let's head out."

Maybe she didn't like the school atmosphere. But the fact that there wasn't an exciting spot around was no reason to expend effort on an expedition in search of pizzazz. Apparently, her goal was to turn this into some kind of fiasco.

"Huh . . . A-am I going too?" Asahina voiced her query in a mournful tone.

"Of course. We can't do anything without the star."

"I-i-in these clothes?"

Asahina was balled up, trembling, in the waitress costume Haruhi brought yesterday.

"Yep, that's right." Haruhi nodded readily.

Asahina hugged herself with a reluctant look on her face.

"Isn't it a pain to keep getting changed? Besides, there might not even be a place for you to change there. So you might as well just wear it the whole time, right? Right? Come on, let's go! Everybody!"

"At least let me wear something over it. . . ."

Asahina's plea was met with . . .

"No."

"But it's so embarrassing."

"It's only embarrassing if you let yourself feel that way! You'll never win a Golden Globe like that!"

Weren't we trying to win first place in the cultural festival best-event poll?

All of the brigade members were assembled in the club room. Koizumi had apparently settled the issues with the script for his class's play and was currently watching Haruhi and Asahina's one-sided exchange. Nagato was also there. And there was a little problem involving Nagato.

". . ."

She was always silent, so I didn't really have any comments regarding that. But she was dressed rather oddly. For some reason, she was once again wearing the witch outfit she had shown us yesterday. You only need to wear it on the day of the festival. Why are you already on standby in the costume?

Haruhi was apparently quite pleased with Nagato's black mantle and pointy hat.

"I'll change your character to an evil alien magician!"

And she was already changing the script. Haruhi looked quite satisfied with Nagato holding the antenna-like pointer with what looked like a star off a Christmas tree attached to the tip. As I watched Nagato gripping the wand, I was finding it hard to argue against the closemouthed book lover being an extraterrestrial evil magician. Seemed to fit her character a lot more than being a terminal for data life forms. She definitely possessed magic-like powers. I'd seen it myself. No doubt about it.

Nagato unexpectedly raised the brim of her hat and looked at me with her usual lifeless eyes.

". . ."

I doubted that it would be okay for Haruhi to arbitrarily use some other class's costume in her movie, but her eyes were utterly devoid of hesitation.

"Kyon! Get the camera ready! Koizumi, you carry the stuff over there. Mikuru, why are you clinging to the desk? Come on, get a move on!"

Asahina's feeble resistance lasted only a moment. Haruhi grabbed the weak waitress by the collar and dragged the squealing little girl to the door. Nagato followed with the hem of her mantle dragging on the floor. Koizumi was the last to disappear into the hallway after winking at me.

As I was wondering if I would have to go with them . . .

"Hey! We can't go film a movie without the cameraman!"

Haruhi's torso stuck through the open door. Her open mouth took up about half of her face as she shouted. I noticed that the band on Haruhi's left arm now read *Great Director,* which only served to depress me.

Looks like she's serious.

The self-proclaimed great director who had yet to film a movie led the way as the beautiful waitress followed with her eyes glued to the ground. The dark-clad witch trailed behind like a shadow. Koizumi carried the paper bag with an easy smile on his face. And I brought up the end, trying to put as much space as possible between me and the band of weirdos. We had already managed to become the center of attention while moving around campus, but this procession that resembled a Halloween party was doing a fine job of attracting interest off campus. Asahina, already the focus of much attention at school, was currently looking down twenty percent of the time, blushing thirty percent of the time, and dragging her feet like a robot fifty percent of the time.

Haruhi was cheerfully humming the melody of the *Heaven and Hell* theme like an impending disaster was on the horizon. No idea where they came from, but she was energetically carrying a yellow megaphone in her right hand and a director's chair in her left, like Mongolian cavalry riding west across the plains. As I wondered where she was planning on making her assault, we arrived at the station. Haruhi bought tickets for all of us and handed them out. She then advanced toward the ticket gate with a prosaic look on her face.

"Wait."

I objected in Asahina's stead, seeing as how she had lost her ability to speak. I pointed to the miniskirted waitress drawing inquisitive glances from every direction and the vertically challenged girl dressed in black standing next to her like an attendant.

"You're going to have them get on the train dressed like this?"

"Something wrong with that?" Haruhi replied, feigning innocence. "You might get arrested if you're running around without anything on, but they're fully dressed. Or what? Would you prefer the bunny-girl outfit? You should have told me earlier then. I wouldn't mind changing it to 'Combat Bunny (Tentative)' if you'd like."

Not sure you should be saying that after dragging her all the way here in a waitress outfit. . . . Anyway, didn't you say that this was the concept for the movie? Not that I would know, but are you supposed to be able to change the concept just like that?

I worked my brain to try to get a glimpse of the feelings of the Creator.

"The most important thing is your ability to adapt to the situation. That's how life on Earth was able to evolve. It's adaptive selection. If you aren't careful, you'll end up eliminated through natural selection. You have to adapt properly!"

Adapt to what? If the environment had a mind of its own, I could see Haruhi being ejected out of the atmosphere.

Koizumi was just smiling and carrying stuff. Nagato was maintaining her silence as mentioned above. Asahina apparently lacked the strength to speak up. Which meant that everyone else was keeping their mouth shut.

I wish someone would do something.

Haruhi apparently took the silence to mean that everyone had been deeply impressed by her words.

"Come on, the train's here. Walk fast, Mikuru. The real stuff's yet to come."

Like a police detective leading away a female perpetrator who had committed a murder for sympathetic reasons, she put her arm around Asahina's shoulders and walked toward the ticket gate.

* * *

And we were there. We got off at the same station as the other day and headed for the same shopping district. I was beginning to have my suspicions when we really did stop in front of the same store as the other day. The electronics store where Haruhi had haggled for the video camera.

"We came as promised!" Haruhi shouted as she cheerfully walked in. The middle-aged guy appeared from the store interior and rested his eyes upon Asahina.

"Ho-ho."

The guy stared at our lead actress with a grin on his face that could only be considered sexual harassment. Asahina was completely motionless, like a fighting-game character after using a super-move.

The guy continued speaking. "Is she the one from yesterday? I didn't recognize her. Ho-ho. Then I'll leave it to you."

Leave what to us? I was in the process of reflexively moving forward to defend the quivering Asahina when Haruhi pushed me back.

"Okay. We're going to have a meeting now, so listen up."

And Haruhi made her announcement with the same smile she'd had right after winning the interclub relay.

"We will now begin shooting the commercial!"

"Th-this store . . . um . . . has a very friendly owner. And he's a nice guy. This store has been around since when it was owned by the grandfather of the current owner, Eijirou. They carry everything from batteries to refrigerators. Um . . . Also, um . . . ," waitress Asahina forcedly recited in a deadpan voice with a twitching smile on her face. Nagato stood next to her holding a placard saying *Ohmori Electronics* as I watched the two of them through the video camera viewfinder.

Asahina had an impressively awkward smile on her face as she held a mike that wasn't actually hooked up to anything.

Koizumi stood next to me holding up cue cards with a faint mocking smile on his face. The cue cards were just a sketchbook Haruhi had scribbled on a moment ago without giving it much thought. Koizumi was flipping through the pages as Asahina went through her lines.

We were in front of the store, still in the shopping district.

Haruhi leaned back in her director's chair with her legs crossed as she watched Asahina's acting with an intense look of concentration on her face.

"Okay, cut!"

She whacked the megaphone against her palm.

"There isn't any emotion. I'm not sure why I can't feel the vibes. It just, like, doesn't have any *oomph* to it," she said while biting her nails.

My reaction as I stopped the video camera was along the lines of "good grief." Asahina also stopped with her hands clutching the mike. Nagato was stationary to begin with. Koizumi just smiled.

Behind us, people passing through the shopping district chattered curiously.

"Mikuru's expression is too stiff. Your smile needs to be more natural. Think happy thoughts. Yeah, aren't you feeling happy right now? You've been handpicked to be the star of the movie. You're never going to experience anything happier in your life!"

I'd really like to tell her to go shove it.

If I had to summarize Haruhi's conversation with the manager from yesterday, it would probably go something like this:

"I'll stick a commercial for this store in the movie, so give me a video camera."

"Sure."

I'm pretty sure there's something wrong with the manager for going along with Haruhi's sweet-talk, but there is definitely something seriously wrong with Haruhi if she's planning on screening a homemade movie with commercials. I've never heard of a leading actress doing a commercial in the middle of a movie. Maybe if you casually sneak something in the background during a scene of the movie, but this is just a feature-length commercial.

"I got it!" Haruhi was shouting to herself.

Could you please stop having these revelations?

"It's kind of odd for a waitress to be at an electronics store."

Weren't you the one who brought the costume?

"Koizumi, hand me that bag. The small one."

Haruhi took the paper bag from Koizumi and grabbed the hand of Asahina, who was looking relieved. Then she barged into the store.

"Manager! Do you have a room in the back we can change in? Yeah, anywhere will do. The bathroom's fine. Really? Then we'll borrow your storeroom."

She casually disappeared into the back of the store with Asahina in tow. It appeared that poor Asahina no longer even had the strength to resist. She obediently allowed herself to be dragged forward by Haruhi's ridiculous strength. It might just have been that she was willing to do anything if it meant getting out of that costume.

The rest of us — Koizumi, Nagato, and I — stood around with nothing to do. Nagato in her black attire hadn't stirred an inch from her position of holding up the placard. She just stared at the video camera. I'm amazed her arms weren't tired.

Koizumi smiled at me.

"It would appear that I won't be making much of an appearance in this film. You see, I'm actually also acting in our class play. It was decided by a class vote. Which means that I am currently struggling to memorize my lines. I would prefer a role in this film with a minimal number of lines. . . . Hey! Why don't you have a go at the lead role?"

"In any case, Haruhi's the one holding authority as far as casting goes. Direct your ideas to her."

"Do you believe me capable of such an incredible task? I, a mere actor, could not possibly bring myself to speak to the producer who is also the director. After all, Suzumiya's orders are absolute. I don't even want to imagine the sort of chastisement she would deliver if I were to disobey her."

Neither do I. Isn't that why I'm being her cameraman? And I'm not even shooting a movie. Just a local commercial film for a private store. The concept of being a good neighbor only goes so far.

The usual frenzied scene was probably occurring in the back of the store right then. The scene of Haruhi stripping a resisting Asahina as she pleased. I didn't know what costume she was putting her in, but she could just wear it herself. She could probably give Asahina a run for her money in the looks department. Did she never consider making herself the star of the movie?

"Sorry for the wait!"

Of the pair walking back out, Haruhi was naturally still in her uniform. The other person's appearance triggered a slide show of images in my mind. Yeah, it's already been six months. Time sure flies. A lot sure has happened in the past six months. Baseball, a remote island, and all kinds of stuff. They're all such fond memories now . . . Like hell they are.

The nostalgic original Mikuru Asahina costume, which Haruhi also wore at the school front gate. The overly revealing costume that became the talk of the school and left Asahina emotionally scarred.

The perfectly flawless bunny girl with flushed cheeks and moist eyes stood wobbling next to Haruhi, bunny ears swaying.

"Yep, absolutely perfect. Guess a bunny girl really is best for promoting merchandise," Haruhi said incomprehensibly as she looked Asahina up and down with a satisfied smile. Asahina seemed completely miserable, as if her spirit were escaping through her half-opened mouth.

"Come on, Mikuru. Do it over from the top. I'm assuming that you've learned your lines by now. Kyon, rewind it to the very beginning."

At this rate, nobody's going to be listening to anything being said. I'm positive that everyone will have their eyes glued to Asahina in her bunny outfit. I hope they don't burn a hole in the screen.

"And take two!" Haruhi shouted with a smack of her megaphone.

The electronics store commercial featuring a half-crying, half-smiling Asahina being completely manipulated by Haruhi was finally finished. It was like watching a foreign wrestler being manipulated by an evil manager.

But then, remember that we'd visited another sponsor earlier. No need to remember, I guess. Haruhi had been planning on another commercial for that sponsor to begin with.

Haruhi was walking through the center of the shopping district as she dragged along the bunny Asahina, who was releasing cute little squeaks and squeals. Trailing behind her like a ghost was Nagato, trudging along expressionlessly in her witch getup. Koizumi and I followed in suit.

My blazer was wrapped around Asahina's shoulders in a feeble attempt to comfort her. It might be making her stand out more, though. This world is full of people with strange tastes. Not that I'm interested in this kind of thing by any means.

We reached the second stop, the model shop, and went through a repetition of the earlier proceedings. With all eyes on her, Asahina turned her teary eyes to me — in other words, the camera — and spoke.

"Th-this model shop was apparently opened last year after Keiji Yamatsuchi, twenty-eight, escaped his life as a white-collar worker. It coincided with his hobby . . . so he just kinda went for it. . . . Sure enough, he hasn't experienced the sales growth he'd like. Growth rate for this year's first term is about eighty percent of what it was for last year's first term. The sales line graph is moving down and right . . . apparently! Everyone be sure to stop by!"

The trembling of Asahina's voice made it sound like she didn't mean a thing she was saying. At any rate, did Yamatsuchi, the manager, even okay this little speech? I'd expect this to just depress him. Who would want to be judged like that by a high school student?

The bunny girl was pointing the assault rifle that had been forced into her hands in an upward direction.

"You mustn't fire this at people. Settle for shooting empty cans or something!"

Nagato was standing behind her holding a placard that read *Yamatsuchi Model Shop* with an unreadable expression on her face. It was a surreal sight. Since Ryoko Asakura looked like a normal person with emotions, I assumed that not all alien-made artificial humans acted like robots. Was Nagato's lack of emotion by design?

Asahina then proceeded to point the rifle at some empty cans on the ground and opened fire.

"Eek —! I'm pretty sure it'll hurt a lot if you get hit. Eek —!"

She even performed a demonstration by fearfully discharging the weapon, riddling the aluminum cans into beehives, which caused a stir among the peanut gallery. Her accuracy was only around ten percent though.

I was feeling pretty guilty about recording this kind of a scene onto a DV cassette tape. I felt like I should apologize to both Asahina and the person who'd developed this technology. He sure didn't invent the video camera to record this crap.

And so we were done for the day once the stupid commercials were finished.

We returned to the school momentarily and lounged around the club room while Haruhi informed us of the schedule for the next stage of filming.

"Tomorrow's Saturday and we have the day off, so we're meeting up in the morning. Be in front of Kitaguchi station at nine. Got it?"

Incidentally, the commercials already ate up fifteen minutes of time. How long would the actual film be? If you screened some three-hour-long epic at a cultural festival, nobody would stick around to the very end. I doubt there'd be much of a turnout either.

I mulled this over in my mind as I watched a discouraged-looking Asahina. She'd been in a waitress outfit for the trip there, and then she'd been forced to wear her bunny-girl outfit on the train for the ride back before finally being allowed to change back into her uniform. She lifelessly collapsed onto the floor. At this rate, we'll have to watch out for the lead actress falling asleep during filming.

I finished off the tea Koizumi had brewed in place of the exhausted Asahina.

"Hey, Haruhi. Can't we do something about Asahina's outfit? There's gotta be something that looks more like something she could actually fight in. Like a combat uniform or camouflage fatigues?" I asked.

Haruhi waved the star-adorned antenna pointer in a reproachful fashion.

"That would kill the surprise when she starts fighting. A waitress doing the fighting gets you the wow factor. Grabbing the audience's attention is key. It's all about concept. Concept!"

Does she even know what "concept" means? I could only sigh.

"Yeah . . . I guess that works, but what's the point in making her come from the future? Would it really matter if she wasn't a time traveler?"

Asahina's shoulders gave a violent shudder where she sprawled. Haruhi didn't even notice or miss a step.

"We can work that all out later on. Just have to come up with an answer when someone brings it up."

Didn't I just bring it up? Give me an answer.

"If you can't come up with an answer, just ignore them! Not like it even matters. It just has to be entertaining!"

"If it's entertaining, sure. And what are the chances that this film you're making will be entertaining? There's no point in filming something that only entertains the director. Are you aiming for a Golden Raspberry nomination in the amateur category?"

"What's that? I'm only after one thing. First place in the cultural festival best-event poll! And if possible, a Golden Globe.

Which is why we need Mikuru to dress appropriately or else people will complain!"

I doubted anybody was going to complain. At any rate, from the look on Haruhi's face, it would seem that the film that had left her enraged had obviously managed to win a Golden Globe at some point in time.

I sighed again and looked to my side. Clad in black, Nagato had parked herself in a corner of the room to engage in her usual reading. Yeah, is she going to die if she doesn't read when she's in this room or something?

"Wait."

I realized something as I watched the book-loving alien.

"Hey, we haven't gotten the script yet."

Actually, we don't even know what the story is yet. All we know is that Asahina is a waitress from the future, Koizumi is a boy esper, and Nagato is an evil alien mage.

"Don't worry."

I had no idea what Haruhi was trying to do, but she suddenly closed her eyes and thrust the tip of the star-adorned pointer at her temple.

"Everything's in here. The script and storyboard are all worked out. You don't have to do any thinking at all. I'll plan out the camera work for you."

Strong words. You're the one who should refrain from thinking and just mindlessly stare out the window. If you had a more reasonable expression on your face, you could trade places with Asahina.

"Tomorrow's the day. Tomorrow! Everyone get psyched up. The first step to winning glory is spiritual fortitude. That's the fastest way to obtaining victory without spending money. Once your soul breaks free of its worldly bonds, latent abilities you never knew about will awaken and release incredible power. That's right!"

Well, I can see that happening when the course of a battle is reversed through some unexpected turn of events in one of those fighting comics, but I'm pretty sure that no matter how much you talk about spiritual fortitude and nationalism, we're a long way from witnessing the Japanese soccer team win the World Cup.

"Then that's it for today! Look forward to tomorrow! Kyon, don't forget about the camera, props, costumes, and other stuff. Make sure you're on time!"

And with that said, Haruhi departed, swinging her bag heroically. As I listened to the *Rocky* theme fade off into the hallway, I bitterly glared at the pile of crap. I wondered which guild I was supposed to report this director's oppression to.

Fact of the matter is, our school life up until this day had consisted of ordinary everyday happenings, with the exception of Haruhi's abnormal passion for filmmaking being on the excessive side. If you went through every single school in the country, you could probably find another group of people doing something similar. Or to put it simply, this was "normal."

No attacks by Nagato's kind. No time traveling with Asahina. No glowing blue mold-like giants showing up. No murders leading to delayed revelations.

This was totally normal school life.

As the countdown to the approaching cultural festival progressed, Haruhi was on a high, riding a steady stream of adrenaline and racing like a pet hamster getting whipped into running Mach 1 on a wheel.

In other words, business as usual.

* * *

— Until this day, that is.

In retrospect, I'd have to say that Haruhi was still holding back. I realized that we had yet to shoot a single frame of the movie. The only footage recorded on the digital videotape was of bunny-girl Asahina promoting the electronics store and plastic model shop in the local shopping district, which only served to get sponsors. Not a glimmer of light had been shed on the film that would be produced, directed, and supervised by Haruhi. We didn't even know the story line yet.

I guess we would have been better off not knowing.

I could have lived with a video of Asahina reporting on the local shopping district. Actually, wouldn't that bring in a bigger audience? It'd also promote the local area. That'd be killing two birds with one stone. Yeah, why don't we just turn it into a Mikuru Asahina promotional video. That'd make me a lot happier. Considering that's my true motive as the cameraman.

Still, I knew that Haruhi would never be satisfied by that. She always carried through on her word. If she said she was gonna do it, she'd do it. She never gave up halfway through. A troublesome case of keeping one's word.

And so, beginning the following day, we would once again find ourselves caught up in some bizarre business. Yeah, seriously. I'm at a loss for words. What was it that Haruhi said again?

Once your soul breaks free of its worldly bonds, latent abilities you never knew about will awaken and release incredible power — or something like that.

I see.

Haruhi?

Why did you have to be the one to one to experience that awakening?

And without you even realizing it.

CHAPTER 3

Saturday. The day of.

We assembled in front of the station. I stuffed an assortment of junk into the largest backpack I could find in our house and walked all the way to the station to find the other four lined up waiting for me.

From a distance, my eyes were drawn to Haruhi in casual dress and Asahina in feminine clothing next to her. Like two sisters who didn't resemble each other the least bit. Asahina was supposed to be the upperclassman here, yet she looked like the younger sister. Only her clothes appeared to be more mature.

Asahina, surrounded by the trio of weirdos, spotted me and waved her hand in a somewhat relieved fashion by way of greeting. Hmm.

"You're late!" Haruhi was yelling, but she looked to be in high spirits again today. She was standing empty-handed because her megaphone and folding director's chair were among my burden of assorted junk.

"It isn't nine o'clock yet," I said sourly as I looked left and right at Nagato's porcelain face and Koizumi's easy smile. "Anyway, Nagato always wears her uniform when we don't have school so that's normal, but why is Koizumi also wearing his uniform?"

"It would appear that this is my costume for the movie."

That was his response.

"That is what I was told yesterday. My role will be that of an esper disguised as an ordinary high school student."

Isn't that exactly what you are?

As I dropped the bag stuffed with the camera and props and wiped off my forehead, Haruhi grinned like a grade-schooler about to go on a field trip.

"Kyon, you were the last to show up so you'll be fined. But not yet. We're taking the bus now. I'll cover the bus fare. Call it a necessary expense. You buy lunch for everyone."

And with that totalitarian decision, she started waving her hand. "Come on, everyone! The bus stop's this way! Get a move on!"

It didn't escape my attention that her armband now read *Super-Director.* Apparently, Haruhi already believed herself beyond a mere great director. She must have had one hell of a movie in mind. I'll say it again: An Asahina promotional video would be far more entertaining to film.

After thirty minutes of bumpy bus riding, we got off at a stop in the hills. Then we spent another thirty minutes laboriously hiking up a steep trail.

It was a commonplace forest park you could find anywhere. Being born and raised around here, I was quite familiar with the area. When I was in grade school, we had a hiking field trip to the nearby hills almost every year.

It was a park in name only — in reality just some cleared-off open space with a fountain tacked on. An utterly empty place that made you want to openly question why a person would voluntarily climb up here. The only happy people I saw around were kids ignorant of pleasure and the family members who'd brought them here.

We set up in a corner of the plaza where the fountain was and designated it as our filming base. Empty-handed, Haruhi looked to be brimming with energy, but I was completely worn out. If I hadn't forced half the stuff onto Koizumi on the way up, I seriously might have collapsed. I leaned against the Wandervogel-issue-looking bag and tried to catch my breath.

"Um, would you like a drink?"

A small plastic bottle was thrust before me. The hand holding the bottle belonged to Asahina.

"If you don't mind that I already drank from it . . ." Oolong tea made for gods. It must taste heavenly. No ifs, ands, or buts about it. If I don't drink it, lightning will strike me down.

As I gladly reached for the offered drink, the evil devil's hand brushed away the angel's arm. Haruhi snatched the oolong tea away from Asahina.

"Save it for later. Mikuru, now isn't the time to be watering the help. We have to hurry or else we might lose this perfect weather. Let's get the camera rolling."

Asahina's eyes opened as wide as saucers.

"What . . . ? We're going to shoot here?"

"Of course we are. Why do you think we came here?"

"Then I don't have to change? Since there isn't a place for me to change around here . . ."

"Sure, there is. Look, there are places all around us."

Haruhi pointed to an area surrounded by a jagged ridge of trees.

"N-n-no — H-help . . ."

Before I had a chance to help, Haruhi disappeared deep into the woods with Asahina in tow.

Once Asahina reappeared, she was clad in the spiffy waitress outfit that would serve as her film attire. Her hair was a tumbled mess as she gazed with quivering eyes at the autumn foliage growing on the side of the road.

One of her eyes was noticeably a different color. Her left eye's blue. What the hell?

"Color contact," Haruhi explained. "It's pretty important to have the left eye be a different color. Look, that's all it takes to add to her mysteriousness. It's all we need to make this work. A symbol of sorts, a symbol."

She grabbed Asahina's chin from behind and tilted her little face. Asahina just looked dumbfounded as she was being manipulated.

"There's a secret in this blue eye," said Haruhi.

"Well, yeah. Wouldn't be much of a story if her eyes were different colors for no reason."

The sight of Asahina's exhausted face was enough to hook me, though.

"So? What's so secret about that color contact?"

"That's still a secret," Haruhi replied with a smirk. "Hey, Mikuru. How long are you going to play dead? Get your act together. You're the leading actress. The most important person after the director and producer. Chin up! Stand up straight!"

"Wah —"

And with a sob, Asahina began posing per Haruhi's instructions. Haruhi forced Asahina to hold the pistol (it's just a model) in her hands.

"Act like you're a female assassin. And make sure people can tell you're from the future."

Just a few of her unreasonable requests. Asahina timidly held the Glock as she glanced sideways at me — the camera — as best as she could. Gotta love how you can feel her pushing herself, yeah. No, I'm serious.

In any case, that freak sure is unnecessarily active. I've seen plenty of bad movies, and I've never thought that I could do a better job so I should make my own film. I wouldn't know how to go about making one anyway. Even if I were to make my own film, I don't entertain the notion that it would be any good. But it would appear that Haruhi seriously believes she has the talent to be a director. At the very least, it's pretty certain that she intends to make something better than those minor films on late-night TV. What exactly does she have to support all that confidence?

Haruhi was yelling as she waved the yellow megaphone around.

"Mikuru! Act less embarrassed! Forget who you are! You just need to become your role! You are no longer Mikuru Asahina! You are Mikuru Asahina!"

. . . Of course, we already knew that there was no basis for Haruhi's confidence. Causing chaos in natural order with groundless confidence was an ability Haruhi was born with. Or else she wouldn't be able to proudly wear that armband and act so high and mighty.

Under director Haruhi's supervision, we began the commemorative shooting of the first scene.

Except that it just consisted of me standing on the side shooting Asahina running across the area. This was supposed to be the opening. She could have at least written a script. But Haruhi said flat-out that no such thing existed.

"It would be bad if I put everything on paper and it got leaked."

That was her reasoning. Looks like we're going to film this movie Hong Kong–style. I was feeling pretty damn exhausted at this point, but when I looked through the camera lens at Asahina dual-wielding pistols, jogging along out of breath, I figured I had it relatively easy.

As the rest of us watched, Asahina continuously ran wearily from right to left until the fifth take when the director finally signaled okay, which was when she collapsed on the ground.

"Ha . . . ha . . ."

Paying no attention to the waitress with both hands on the ground as her back rose and fell with each breath, Haruhi directed her next instruction to Nagato, waiting on the sidelines.

"Okay, we're doing Yuki and Mikuru's battle scene next."

Nagato, in her favorite black outfit, slowly moved in front of the camera. The outfit was just a pitch-black mantle over her uniform and a black pointy hat on her head, so there was no need for her to be dragged into the thicket like Asahina, fortunately. Then again, Nagato would probably be fine with changing her clothes anywhere. Why don't we reverse their roles? Make Nagato the waitress and Asahina the mage. That would be curiously appropriate.

Haruhi had Asahina and Nagato stand facing each other three meters apart.

"Mikuru, unload like crazy on Yuki."

"Huh," Mikuru responded. She shook her hair, which was a tangled mess after all that running. "But I'm not supposed to fire this at people . . ."

"It's fine. With your aim, you won't hit her much anyway. Even if you were able to hit her, Yuki could probably just dodge it."

Nagato just stood silently with the star-tipped pointer in hand.

Well yeah, I'd have to agree there. Nagato could have a gun pressed against her forehead and still manage to dodge the bullet.

"Um . . ."

Looking like a newly hired waitress having to report a broken dish to the scary chef, Asahina nervously glanced up at Nagato.

"It's fine," replied Nagato. And with a spin of the pointer, she said, "Shoot me."

"See, she says it's fine. Fire away. And just a heads-up, you don't fire both at the same time. You alternate. That's a basic principle of dual-wielding pistols."

Koizumi was holding the reflector board above his head. Haruhi brought it from who knows where. The photography club might be reporting a theft right about now.

"Anyway, Koizumi, aren't you the leading man?"

"One must adapt to the circumstances as they change. I'm more disposed to being on this side of the camera. I've been thinking since yesterday about a way to remain backstage . . ."

"Unh!"

Asahina, straining to hold up the pistols, fired rapidly with her eyes shut tight. And I stood to the side filming that sight. I couldn't really see the BB trails, but considering that Nagato was standing completely still without even a flicker of emotion across her face, I guess she really wasn't scoring any hits. Maybe she's using magic . . . or so I was thinking when Nagato slowly raised the pointer and whirled it before her face. Bullets began falling to the ground with a clatter. Even without glasses, her vision was as incredible as ever.

Nagato was staring at the muzzle without a single blink. Not that she blinked much to begin with, but then again, blinking just because "it would be unnatural if I didn't blink once in a while" would feel even more unnatural. Whether she was walking around with her pupils wide open, breaking through ceilings, or teleporting around, I would no longer be surprised. Which was why I wasn't surprised right then.

Nagato waved the pointer sporadically like a broken windshield wiper and with each swing, BBs fell with a clatter.

In any case, this sure was a boring battle scene. Nagato was only waving her wand around and Asahina was only firing those two Glocks or Berettas or whatever. And she wasn't hitting anything. First off, Haruhi only told her to "unload like crazy" and didn't give her any lines to say. All we could hear was Asahina moaning and wailing in her little, lovely voice.

The whole thing felt more like a halfhearted battle scene between a viper and mongoose who had agreed to avoid any fatal blows beforehand.

"Yeah, that should do it."

Once Asahina had run out of bullets, Haruhi tapped her shoulder with the megaphone. I lowered the video camera and approached Haruhi, sitting cross-legged on the director's chair.

"Hey, Haruhi. How is this a movie? I have no idea what the story is about."

Super-director Suzumiya gave me a side glance.

"That's fine. I planned on having a lot of cut-and-paste work done during the editing phase anyway."

Who's going to be doing it? That cut-and-paste work. I have a feeling the word "editing" has been included in my list of duties.

"At least put in some lines," I suggested.

"We can just remove the noise and dub over later if we have to. We're going to have to add sound effects and background music. There's no need to think too much about it at this point!"

Well, yeah. Considering that the story's only in your head at this point, there's nothing for us to think about. At the very least,

I have to take care to keep Haruhi's sexual harassment of Asahina to a bare minimum. No other males are allowed to touch her body. That's where I draw the line. No one's got a problem with that, right?

"Let's move on to the next scene, then! Time for Yuki's counterattack. Yuki, wreck Mikuru with your magic!"

Nagato's eyes, darker than her costume, turned to me from under the brim of her black hat. Her head tilted at an angle only I could distinguish. I basically got the message. Nagato was asking if it was okay.

No! was the obvious response. Magic aside, I couldn't give permission to hurt Asahina in any way. Look, she's all pale and trembling.

Of course, Haruhi had no idea that Nagato could use incomprehensible, spontaneous magic. She just wanted her to *act* like she was using magic.

Nagato appeared to understand and, while remaining completely silent, raised the antenna pointer and began waving it around the way audience members at a concert wave glow sticks.

"That's good enough," said Haruhi. "We'll add visual effects to this scene. Kyon, make it so there are beams shooting out of Yuki's wand later."

How am I supposed to add in effects like that? I don't have the ability. If you're planning on borrowing staff and equipment from Industrial Light & Magic, though, that's a different story.

"That's when Mikuru should scream! And then fall down in pain."

After a moment of nervous hesitation, Asahina murmured, ". . . Eek," before suddenly falling straight onto her face. Nagato stood next to a fallen Asahina like the Grim Reaper come to claim her soul. I stood filming the whole scene while Koizumi stood next to me, still holding up the reflector board.

The stares from all of the families around us were starting to hurt.

Having been granted a brief respite in a most compassionate act by Haruhi, we sat in a ring on the ground.

Haruhi was replaying the film I had shot with a deliberate look on her face as she nodded to herself.

A number of children had scurried in between Asahina and Nagato and were asking questions like, "What show is this for?" Asahina shook her head with a weak smile while Nagato completely ignored them, becoming one with the land.

I had no idea what kind of scenes the footage I was taking would be used for since Haruhi refused to tell us, but the super-director informed us that we would be going to a nearby shrine next. Break's over already, huh?

"There are doves there."

That's the case, apparently.

"We're going to film Mikuru walking with doves flying all around in the background. I'd prefer doves that are completely white, but I'm willing to take any color at this point."

I was pretty sure we were only going to find typical park doves. With her arm linked in the already worn-out Asahina's arm (so she wouldn't be able to run away), Haruhi walked through the forest park toward the street. Koizumi and I divided up the equipment and followed like local Sherpas trailing a film crew doing a piece on the jungle. We eventually arrived at a large shrine in the middle of the mountains. I hadn't been there in a while. Not since a field trip in grade school.

Haruhi stood in front of a sign on the grounds that said *Do not feed* while spreading bread crumbs like she was trying to make flowers bloom on a wilted tree. I guess she can't read.

All at once the ground was covered by a swarm of doves, endlessly dropping from the sky. The sight of the shrine grounds covered in doves was quite disturbing. Asahina was standing alone within the carpet of doves. The waitress stood, lip trembling, with her feet being pecked. I was filming the scene from the front. What the hell was I doing?

Offscreen, Haruhi raised the Eagle or Tokarev or whatever kind of gun it was she had taken from Asahina and flipped off the safety. I was wondering what she was doing when she suddenly fired at Asahina's feet.

"Ahh —"

Never thought I'd actually get to see doves getting whacked by a peashooter. The act of violence, enough to make the SPCA come flying in, sent the symbols of peace fluttering and shrieking.

"This is it! This is the shot I wanted! Kyon, make sure you're filming this!"

I suppose that since the camera was running, I was technically filming. Asahina was hunched over with her hands over her head within the swirl of doves flying in all directions.

"Come on, Mikuru! You're supposed to walk toward us while the doves are flying in the background! Stand up!"

It didn't look like we'd have time to shoot such a scene. As I gazed through the viewfinder, I could see that in the background, a priest from the shrine had come flying in the SPCA's stead. He was wearing a hakama, so it'd be safe to assume he was affiliated with the shrine. I was preparing for a stern lecture or two when Haruhi, without a moment's hesitation, resorted to drastic measures.

With the CZ or SIG or whatever model gun in hand, she aimed at the old man and opened fire. The priest (probably) began dancing like he was standing on a hot iron plate. The AARP's going to come calling next.

"Retreat!"

And with that cry, Haruhi quickly turned and sprinted off. No idea when Nagato had made her move, but she was already waiting for us under the gate in the distance. Asahina would probably be too slow to escape if we left her by herself, so Koizumi and I each grabbed an arm and carried her off with the rest of the equipment.

The director had already run away. We couldn't leave the leading lady behind to be the scapegoat.

Ten minutes later, we were sitting in the corner of some kind of roadside restaurant. We were having lunch, and for some reason I had to pay for it.

"That might have been a waste. It might have been a better ad lib to just pretend that the old priest was an enemy and beat the crap out of him."

Haruhi was babbling on about borderline criminal activity.

Once Asahina had sucked in a whole three noodles of her zaru soba, she collapsed face-forward on the table.

"Mikuru. You don't eat much, huh? You'll never grow like that. Only your breasts are growing. That'll only satisfy a group of hard-core freaks. You need to grow taller, too."

While she was saying that, Haruhi was stealing Asahina's noodles and scarfing them down.

I already know. I don't know how many years it will be, but Asahina will grow to have a face and body that could represent the whole solar system. She doesn't know that, though.

Koizumi had a mocking smile on his face. Nagato tacitly moved assorted sandwiches to her mouth and chewed.

I pushed my empty plate of spaghetti to the side and spoke to Haruhi, with two people's lunches before her.

"What are you going to do if that priest complains to the school? Koizumi's uniform made it pretty obvious where we were from."

"It'll probably be fine." Haruhi was ridiculously optimistic. "It was fairly far away and the blazer's pretty common. If he does complain, we just have to play dumb. Pretend it was someone else. BBs aren't enough to prove anything."

I stared at the video camera containing the incriminating evidence. I'm pretty sure that the second this is screened, the cat will be out of the bag. I doubt there is another waitress in the area willing to go to a shrine to be surrounded by doves.

"So? Where are we going next?"

"We'll go back to the park. On second thought, that wasn't enough to be a battle. We'll need more intense action to grip the audience's hearts. Yeah, I can picture it already. Mikuru, running frantically around the forest, pursued by Yuki. And then Mikuru falls off a cliff. That's when Koizumi, who happens to be passing by, saves her. How's that sound?"

Pretty haphazard turn of events. What kind of high school student would happen to be walking by in the middle of these mountains in his uniform? Pretty damn suspicious. And I had a feeling Haruhi really intended to shove Asahina off a cliff. Yeah, Haruhi, you should take the fall. Put on the costume and act as Asahina's stunt double. Well, you're missing a bit around the chest area. . . .

As I was pondering such matters, Haruhi raised her eyebrows and gave me a sideways look.

"Are you thinking about something else? You had better not be picturing me in the waitress outfit."

What an accurate guess.

"I'm the director. I can't just merrily step in front of the camera. If you try to chase a couple of rabbits, you'll end up tripping over a stump and falling down."

"Aren't you also supposed to be the producer?"

"There's nothing wrong with undertaking multiple backstage roles. Still, it might be nice to show up on camera for a brief cameo appearance. Adding some fun tidbits will hook those hard-core fans."

What kind of fans are you aiming for? Asahina fans? At this point, this is nothing more than an Asahina costume collection. . . . On second thought, that's good enough.

Koizumi returned his café au lait to the table with an elegant motion. "Are the three of us the only ones who will be appearing in the movie?"

Idiot. Don't ask unneeded questions.

"That's right. . . ."

Haruhi puckered her lips like a duck's bill and became deeply engrossed in thought. You should think this kind of stuff out beforehand.

"Three people might be too few. Yeah, it's not enough. Supporting characters are what allow the main characters to truly shine. Koizumi, excellent pickup. To show my appreciation, I'll increase your screen time."

"Why . . . thank you very much."

Koizumi remained smiling, though his face had an *oops* look on it. Serves you right. Let sleeping dogs lie. I kept my mouth shut.

But where did she intend to find new characters? There was a seventy-five percent chance that anyone she brought in at random would have some kind of twisted backstory. Based on progression, a slider would probably be next. And I sure didn't want one of those to show up in our world.

"You have to beat up a bunch of underlings before you can defeat the last boss. Underlings, underlings . . ."

I glanced at Haruhi, fingers stroking her lower lip.

"They should be good enough."

I read Haruhi's mind. Taniguchi and Kunikida. The only two people I can live with her bringing in at this point. Less significant than supporting characters. True underlings. They're less harmless than a healer slime showing up alone.

"That works."

I averted my eyes from the face of the director, looking like she wanted one more person, to steal a glance at Asahina with her eyes shut and her cheek on the table. She's even cute when she's asleep. Even if she's faking it.

I turned to look at Nagato, slurping her soda in that Grim Reaper getup. Once I was done observing her utter lack of emotion, I turned back to Haruhi.

"So? What's next? What are we filming?"

Haruhi slowly gulped down the soba broth, buying herself the time it took until it finished. Once she was done, she spoke.

"In any case, we need something bad to happen to Mikuru. A poor little girl undergoes ordeal after terrible ordeal until she finally gets her happy ending. That's the theme of this movie. The more Mikuru suffers, the more impact the final catharsis will have. Don't worry, Mikuru. The movie has a happy ending."

The ending will be the only happy part. In the meantime, Asahina has to suffer director Haruhi's abuse. Well then, I wonder what kind of scenario Haruhi has prepared. Since I appear to be the only restraint on Haruhi, I'll need to pay extra special attention. By the way, what's a catharsis?

Asahina's closed eyes were now half-open and looking at me, pleading for help. A case of heterochromia where only her left eye was blue. However, she quickly released a soft sigh and her eyes slowly closed. What is this? Are you saying that you can't rely on me?

Since Koizumi and Nagato won't serve as any sort of obstruction at this point, I'm your only ally here.

Of course, it's not like I've had any success trying to stop Haruhi in the past six months. I wish she'd at least accept my chivalrous intentions. Though I can't deny that this feels about as empty as throwing a lance at a windmill.

To be honest, I was wondering if I should even stop her. Half a year ago, I felt that I absolutely had to stop her from founding the SOS Brigade, even if I had to tie her arms behind her back. In the end, while I was dillydallying around, Haruhi went ahead and prepared a room and members. Little by little, I also ended up as one of the members . . . which brings us to our current situation.

Still, if I had whacked her in the back of the head with a stick or jumped her or ambushed her and managed to stop her, I might not have met Asahina or Nagato or Koizumi. Or we would have met under different circumstances. Which means I wouldn't have known about unbelievable things like aliens and time travelers. We would just pass each other in the hallway as classmates or total strangers.

Don't ask me which way would have been better. I've already heard self-promotion spiels from the other three members, and I've already been witness to Nagato's weird power, the other Asahina, and Koizumi turning into a red ball. If we went to some parallel world, you could probably find a version of me that hasn't spoken a word with Haruhi or the other three, so go ahead and ask him. I don't have an answer.

But I had to come up with an answer in this current situation. Filmmaking. Hmm. An appropriate cultural festival activity.

Nothing wrong with that. The only thing weird would be inside Haruhi's head, but at this point that would come as a surprise to nobody. As far as I'm concerned, Haruhi spontaneously babbling about wanting to make a movie could be considered routine work. Just wing it and things will work themselves out —

At least, that's what I thought. That's why I didn't bother trying to stop filming the movie. Be a director or whatever you want. Abuse everyone around you to your heart's content. If that's what makes you happy, I'll smother my internal sighing and go along with it. Because by all means, I sure as hell don't want to be locked up alone with you in some weird dimension again.

As I watched a psyched-up Haruhi, an exhausted Asahina, a smiling Koizumi, and a poker-faced Nagato, that's how I felt.

Not knowing that I would later regret not stopping her.

We returned to the forest park. Can't you work on the scheduling some more? We should have finished the filming before we ran off to the shrine. The problem was that the script only existed inside Haruhi's head. It's important to write things down. The written word is a wonderful thing.

"Forget the guns. I was expecting more impressive bullets, but it doesn't make an impression without any flashy smoke or sounds. Doesn't seem to be working at all. I guess fake isn't good enough."

As Haruhi made remarks that would only send Yamatsuchi Model Shop's business further into the red, she used the tips of her sneakers to draw two crosses on the ground. Looks like those are where Asahina and Nagato are supposed to stand.

"Mikuru's over here. Yuki's here."

"Wah."

After being dragged around by Haruhi the whole morning, Asahina was looking like she'd already burned up a day's worth of calories, no longer having the energy to resist. Wandering around in that sexy-waitress outfit must have taken a serious toll on her spirit. She could no longer feel shame, having regressed to an infantile mind state, acting like a doll.

Nagato acted like a doll to begin with. She moved silently to her assigned position with her black mantle fluttering in a mountain breeze.

Haruhi twirled around her finger the model gun she had taken from Asahina.

"Don't move from that position. I want a scene of the two of you glaring at each other. Koizumi, get the reflector board ready."

And then Haruhi, having returned to the director's chair, pointed the gun at the sky and opened fire.

"Action!" she yelled.

I raised the camera, flustered, but Asahina was probably even more flustered. Action? Haruhi only told her to stand still. What kind of action was supposed to happen here?

". . ."

Nagato and Asahina wordlessly gauged each other's expressions.

"Um . . ."

Asahina was the first to look away.

". . ."

Nagato continued to stare at Asahina.

". . ."

Asahina also fell silent.

And for a while, the two just continued staring at each other as a soft breeze blew by.

"Geez!"

Haruhi snapped for some reason.

"You can't have a battle like that!"

Since they're just standing there.

Haruhi, now holding the megaphone instead of a gun, stomped over to Asahina and began pounding the chestnut braids she had tied.

"Mikuru, listen up. You can't just relax because you happen to be cute. There are more than enough girls out there who get by just by being cute. If you let loose for just a bit, those younger girls will pass you by in no time."

What are you trying to say?

Haruhi continued lecturing Asahina, covering her head.

"That's why, Mikuru. At least fire a beam from your eye!"

"Huh?"

Asahina opened her eyes in surprise.

"That's impossible!"

"It's why your left eye is a different color. It isn't blue for no reason. There is supposed to be incredible power hidden within. That's where the beam comes in. Mikuru Beam. Shoot."

"I-I can't!"

"Try harder!"

Haruhi had the slumped Asahina in a headlock and was whacking the back of her head with the yellow megaphone.

The sight of Asahina crying out in pain was too much for me to bear. I handed the camera to Koizumi, who had set down the reflector board to enjoy the scene, and grabbed Haruhi by the collar.

"Cut it out, moron."

I peeled the tyrannical super-director off the small waitress.

"Normal humans can't possibly fire beams from their eyes. Are you an idiot?"

Look at Asahina, covering her head with her arms. The poor thing's on the verge of tears. Just look at those pearls dripping from her round eyes.

"Hmph."

Haruhi, still in my grip, turned to the side and sniffed. "I obviously know that much."

I released my grip. Haruhi tapped the back of her neck with the megaphone.

"I was telling her to use as much effort as it would take to shoot out beams. Since she has so little drive, it's hard to believe she's the leading actress. You really can't take a joke, can you?"

The problem would be that your jokes end up being anything but. What if Asahina really ends up being able to fire beams?

. . . She can't, right?

Worried, I gave Asahina a sideways glance. She looked up at me with tears flowing from her heterochromatic eyes, then blinked and tilted her head. It would appear that my eye contact didn't get the message through to her. That was when Koizumi popped out and admonished Haruhi.

"Perhaps we can use CG effects after we're done filming to handle that section."

Koizumi, with a tissue box in hand, flashed a friendly smile like a con artist and handed the box to Asahina.

"Wasn't that your intention to begin with, Suzumiya?"

"It sure was," said Haruhi.

Sure it was, I thought.

Asahina wiped away her tears with the tissues and blew her nose while looking suspiciously at Haruhi and me.

Nagato remained standing in the wind, looking like an overly conspicuous stagehand. Can't the sun set already? I can't wait for it to become too dark to film anymore.

"That was no good. We're doing a retake," Haruhi said and began brainstorming a signature pose with Asahina. "Put your hand like this as you shout '*Mikuru Beam!*'"

"Something like this . . . ?"

"No, like this! And shut your right eye."

Apparently, a beam fires from her eye when her left hand displays a victory sign next to her left eye while winking.

"Mikuru, try saying it."

". . . Mi-Mi-Mi-, Mikuru Beam!"

"Louder!"

"Mikuru Beam!"

"Don't be shy about it!"

"Hee . . . Mikuru Bea . . . m!"

"Shout from your belly!"

Is this some kind of comedy act?

Asahina was shouting until she was red, coerced into diaphragmatic breathing by Haruhi. The stares from the wandering kids and families around were painful. I wanted to tell them that this wasn't a show for them to watch, but since we were shooting a movie, we were technically putting on a show. Maybe we could just film the making of scenes. I don't know what a Haruhi-style happy story would be like, but we've got more than enough for a Mikuru Asahina promo.

Eventually, Asahina and Nagato were back standing on their respective cross marks, Koizumi was holding the reflector board in a touchdown signal, Haruhi was reclined next to him, and I had circled around two meters behind Nagato, garbed in black, to film Asahina over her shoulder. This camera angle was per Haruhi's instructions.

An abrupt transformation soon followed.

"Okay, fire the beam now!"

In response to Haruhi's shout, Asahina uncertainly struck a pose.

"Mi . . . Mikuru Beam!" she shouted adorably in a forced falsetto with an obvious look at the camera.

In that instant, the camera viewfinder suddenly went pitch dark.

"Ah?"

I couldn't understand what had happened. I thought the camera had malfunctioned. I removed my eye from the finder to find an ominous-looking black pointy hat.

". . ."

Nagato had her hand in a fist before my eyes. Nagato's right hand had covered the lens and made it dark.

"Huh?" said Haruhi, whose mouth was wide open.

The cross mark Haruhi had drawn was two meters in front of me. Nagato had been standing there just a moment ago. When Haruhi had yelled action and Asahina had shouted, Nagato's black silhouette had definitely shown up on camera. And not even a second later, Nagato was, for some reason, standing silently with one arm raised, gripping something in front of my face. The only explanation I had was that she warped.

"What?" Haruhi said. "Yuki, when did you get over there?"

Nagato didn't respond, but instead kept her bead-like eyes on Asahina. As for Asahina, she had her eyes open wide in surprise. And then she slowly blinked —

Nagato's hand once again moved at the speed of light. She made a grabbing motion in the air as though she were catching a mosquito. What happened to the star-tipped antenna she was supposed to carry?

Huh? I just heard a weird noise. Like a lit match falling into a ditch with running water. A sound like that.

"Huh . . . ?"

The puzzled voice belonged to Asahina. She must not understand the situation. I don't either. What's Nagato trying to do?

Asahina, seeking salvation, turned to the side — and an unnatural sound came from where Koizumi was. A sound that could not be mistaken, like air escaping from a punctured tire. . . .

The reflector board that had been raised above Koizumi's head — just a cheap piece of Styrofoam covered by a sheet of thick white paper — had been severed at a diagonal angle. Koizumi, at a loss for words for once, stood stunned as he watched the top half of the reflector board slide off. But I didn't have the time to enjoy such a rare sight.

Nagato moved. Nagato alone.

A dark shadow leapt from the ground and landed right in front of Asahina. Nagato's right hand reached out from under her black mantle and grabbed Asahina's face. Her slender fingers covered Asahina's eyes, and her fingertips drove into Asahina's temples.

"Ahh . . . Na-Na-Na-Nagato . . ."

Nagato paid no heed and threw the star waitress to the ground. Looking like the Grim Reaper riding on top of that ample bosom. Asahina screamed and grabbed Nagato's slender arms, locked in an iron grip.

"Ah!"

I finally came to my senses. What was that? It looked like Nagato had teleported over to interfere with the filming, but then Koizumi's reflector board split in half, and then the alien attacked the time traveler. When did Haruhi tell the two of them to act out this scene — or I guess that's not possible. The director, along with Koizumi and me, was also at a loss. And the two of them didn't look like they were acting.

". . . Cut, cut!"

Haruhi stood up and whacked her chair with the megaphone.

"Hey, Yuki. What are you doing? That wasn't part of the plan."

Nagato remained silent, riding on the struggling Asahina, whose white thighs were half-exposed.

Upon hearing a soft murmur, I turned to find Koizumi staring at the severed edge of the reflector board with a grimace on his face. He then noticed my gaze and gave me a strange look. What's that supposed to mean?

Or no, who cares about Koizumi's meaningful looks. Right now, I have to do something about Nagato's all-out martial arts antics. I ran, with camera in hand, toward the jumbled waitress and black-garbed mage.

"What are you doing? Hey, Nagato."

The wide-brimmed hat slowly turned toward me. Nagato's black-hole-like eyes looked up at me and her thin lips parted.

". . ."

My expectations that she would say something were shot. Nagato silently shut her mouth with a look on her face suggesting that she couldn't find the appropriate words for this situation, before gradually standing up from the mount position. With a jerk of her black-mantled right shoulder, her arm withdrew under her outfit.

"Hah . . . Hah . . ."

Asahina was lying on the ground faceup, trembling in fear. Well, yeah, of course she's scared. If Nagato charged over with that emotionless look and threw me to the ground, I'd be shaking in my boots. Especially since in her current getup, she looks like some kind of dark wizard that you really wouldn't want to bump into in the middle of the night. Might even make some fainthearted preschooler wet his pants.

". . ."

Nagato, eyes covered by the oversize pointy hat, didn't move an inch. She just stared at me.

I gently helped the sniffling Asahina stand up. The sight of those long eyelashes, bordering gorgeous eyes brimming with tears, only served to make her even more attractive . . . Huh?

"Man, what are the two of you doing? Please don't do stuff that isn't in the script."

The director who hadn't even written down the script walked over and went "Huh?" in a dubious voice, just as I had.

"Mikuru, what happened to the contact?"

"What . . ."

Asahina, clinging to my arms in tears, moved her finger below her left eye.

"Huh?"

The three of us could only stand around looking puzzled. In these situations, you're supposed to consult the person who has a firm grasp on the situation.

"Nagato, do you know what happened to Asahina's color contact?"

"Don't know," Nagato replied in a flat voice. Pretty sure she's lying.

"Maybe it fell out during the tussle," Haruhi guessed incorrectly and began searching the ground. "Kyon, you help look. That wasn't cheap. It cost quite a bit."

I joined the scampering Haruhi and got on all fours. Even though I told her it was useless. I had a feeling that I'd seen Nagato's right hand holding something when she got off Asahina. And that hand had been attached to Asahina's face when they were tangled together.

"Why can't we find it anywhere?"

My apologies to the duck-billed Haruhi, but I wasn't looking very hard. I turned to find Koizumi playing with the pieces of the reflector board, attaching and separating them. You pretend to look, too.

Koizumi smiled.

"It may have blown away in the wind. Since it's light."

He was saying irresponsible things as he displayed the remains of the reflector board.

Haruhi jumped up and took them from him. "What happened? It split in half? Hmm, it was cheap anyway. Well, can't expect anything more from our photography club. Koizumi, tape it back together in the back."

And with those careless remarks, she turned her crocodile-like gaze back to Asahina, who was spaced out after having finally stopped crying.

"We can't continue filming without the color contact. What do we do?"

She appeared to be thinking. Eventually, she snapped her fingers as though a lightbulb had gone off in her head.

"That's it. We'll say that the eye color changes after she transforms."

"T-transforms?" said Asahina.

"That's right! It wouldn't be very realistic if you were always wearing that costume. That costume will be what you're wearing after you transform. You'll usually be wearing a more normal outfit."

There's something wrong with people trying to make fiction too realistic, plus I think she just admitted that dressing up as a waitress wasn't normal.

Asahina was rapidly nodding her head up and down. "I-is that really okay? I really want to wear normal clothes. Really."

"Which is why Mikuru's normal outfit will be a bunny girl!"

"Huh? Wh-wh-wh-why?"

"Because that's the only one I brought. Your usual regular clothing would look too dull on the screen. Wait! I just came up with a backstory. Basically, Mikuru normally acts as a bunny girl attracting customers for the shopping district. When she senses danger, she immediately transforms! She turns into a combat waitress. Well, isn't that perfect?"

Didn't you just say something about being realistic?

"Then let's get started."

Haruhi smiled a dangerous smile that looked like a crescent moon as she pinned Asahina's arms behind her back. "Ow, ow, ow," cried the waitress as she was taken into the woods.

Hmm.

. . . Well, I guess that's fine. I can only pray for Asahina, but it is very convenient for me if Haruhi runs off right now. Her sacrifice will not be wasted. And I can't wait to see her in a bunny suit.

. . . And that worked out well since I had something to ask Nagato.

"So what was with the improvisation back there?"

Nagato impassively pressed down on the brim of the pointy hat, leaving most of her face covered by its shadow, and slowly extended her right hand. The outfit was just something on top of her uniform, so her right sleeve was that of a sailor uniform. She then flipped her right index finger so it was facing upward. A blue contact lenses was resting atop it.

So you snatched it after all.

"Here," Nagato murmured. "Laser."

And with that, she shut her mouth.

". . ."

You know, it's been on my mind for a while, but your explanations don't even satisfy the bare-minimum requirements. You could at least try talking for ten seconds at a time.

Nagato stared at her own finger.

"Invisible coherent light possessing a high level of directivity."

She spoke in an excruciatingly slow voice. I see. Invisible coherent light . . .

Sorry, I know even less now.

"Laser?" I said.

"Yes," said Nagato.

"That's quite a surprise," chimed in Koizumi. He picked up the contact in his fingers and observed it through the light. "It looks like an ordinary contact lens."

He sounds like he's really impressed. I couldn't figure out what to be surprised about, let alone be impressed.

"What's this all mean?"

Koizumi chuckled.

"Could you show us your right palm? No, not you. Nagato."

The black-garbed girl directed her gaze to me as though she were asking for permission, so I nodded. Upon confirmation, she unclenched the remaining three fingers and thumb on her hand, at which point I stopped breathing.

". . ."

A gust of silence blew around the three of us. I shivered and finally understood. *So that's what it was.*

Nagato's plain right palm was riddled with a number of small, black burned holes. They looked like they were the product of stabbing by red-hot tongs. There were five of them.

"I didn't have time to shield."

Don't act so unconcerned about it. It looks damn painful.

"Very powerful. Happened in an instant."

"So the laser beam came from Asahina's left eye?" asked Koizumi.

"Yes."

Don't just say yes. Same goes for you, Koizumi. There's something that needs to be done before we figure out the situation.

"I will commence restoration shortly."

True to her words, the holes in Nagato's hand were swiftly covered by her original white skin, right before our eyes.

"What the hey?"

I could only groan.

"Was Asahina seriously firing beams from her eyes?"

"Not a particle projection cannon. Concentrated light."

Big difference. A laser or maser or the Markalite FAHP all look the same to an amateur. Like I'm going to know the difference between an ion cannon and an antiproton cannon. Who cares how it works as long as it blows up monsters.

"The problem here would be that Asahina has been shooting off heat rays without any monsters around."

"Not heat rays. Photon laser."

Like I said, big difference. We don't need scientific verification.

Nagato fell silent and closed her right hand. I covered my head with my arms while Koizumi flicked the contact.

"Was this an ability Asahina was previously capable of?"

"No," Nagato replied instantly. "At the present, Mikuru Asahina is a normal human being. Her makeup is similar to that of ordinary people."

"So there's something special about this color contact?" Koizumi offered.

"No. It is a mere decoration."

Thought so. After all, Haruhi was the one who brought it. Actually, that's the biggest problem here. The fact that she, and nobody else, was the one who brought it.

There was something that needed to be emphasized. If Nagato hadn't covered me, Asahina's laser beam would have gone through the video camera lens, through my eyeball, burning up a number of things, before finally exiting the back of my skull. Pretty sure my brains would have been smoking. That'd be bad, yeah.

Still, it feels like Nagato's always saving my life. Pretty embarrassing.

"Which means . . ."

Koizumi smiled grimly as he stroked his chin.

"This is Suzumiya's doing, isn't it? She wanted there to be a Mikuru Beam, and reality was altered to accommodate that. That's how it appeared."

"Yes."

Nagato gave confirmation without a hint of emotion on her face. I wasn't able to stay so calm.

"Hold on. There isn't any magic or whatever in the contact, right? How can it fire killer rays just because Haruhi wished for it?"

"Suzumiya doesn't need magic or unknown technology. If she believes something to exist, then it actually does."

Don't expect your bullshit reasoning to convince me.

"Haruhi didn't seriously mean to shoot beams when she said that. That was just within the movie. Even *she* said that it was just a joke, didn't she?"

"Indeed."

Koizumi also nodded. Don't just accept my objection. Now I can't keep going.

"We are also aware that Suzumiya possesses common sense. However, it is also a fact that the common sense of this world does not apply to her. This incident is most likely the result of some kind of extraordinary phenomenon. That would be . . . Oh, they've come back. We shall continue this later."

Koizumi casually slipped the contact into his shirt pocket.

What a pain.

Use wit and tact to save the world from destruction, beat the crap out of bad guys, no questions asked, hold limited ESP battles within a conveniently small world, and throw in some random human melodrama. . . .

Fact of the matter is, I'd prefer it that way. If I have to be dragged into a world that sounds like it's out of fiction, give me something that's way out there. The more removed from reality, the better.

But look at me now. Talking to a certain classmate resulted in disaster, I'm surrounded by a bunch of people with backgrounds I completely don't understand, and we're doing stuff I can't even begin to try to comprehend. Shooting beams from eyes? What's with that? What's the point of trying?

On second thought, not a single member of the mysterious trio of Asahina, Nagato, and Koizumi has actually proven their identity. All of them delivered their little introductions, but I'm still not crazy enough to buy their crap. Not even after being involved in all those incidents that might suggest otherwise. Everything has its standards, and I've got my own set of them. Though they're starting to get out of whack.

According to these people, first off, Asahina was a time traveler from the future. She wouldn't tell me what year she was from, but I knew why she was here. To observe Haruhi Suzumiya.

Nagato was an alien-made humanoid interface. Don't start going, "What's that?" That was my reaction too, so we're even. As for why something like that is on Earth, it's because Nagato's superiors, the Data Overmind or whatever, apparently have an interest in Haruhi Suzumiya.

And then Koizumi was an esper dispatched from some mysterious organization known as the "Agency." One of his missions was to transfer to this school, and his job was to monitor Haruhi Suzumiya.

As for Haruhi herself, surrounded by three people with such bizarre profiles, her identity is still the greatest mystery. According to Asahina, she was a "time warp." Nagato said she was the "potential for evolution." Koizumi went so far as to call her "God."

Seriously, good work, everyone.

And while you're at it, do something about Haruhi. Or the female brigade chief will remain a mystery and I'll remain trapped in her neutron-star-level gravitational field. I can live with it for now, but, you know, try to picture how it'll be ten years from now. What are we supposed to do if Haruhi's still Haruhi? That'll be pretty ugly. Illegally occupying club rooms, prowling the streets with the eyes of a predator, going berserk while causing a ruckus, and unstable mood swings can be forgiven when you're still a teenager. Not the actions of a grown adult. She'd just be a social misfit. Do Asahina, Koizumi, and Nagato still intend to go along with Haruhi at that point?

As for me, I'll apologize first. Sorry, I don't have any intention of tagging along. Because time is unforgiving. Life doesn't have reset buttons falling out of the sky, and you're not going to find save points marked on the side of the road.

It doesn't matter if Haruhi distorted time, caused an explosion of data, or created and destroyed worlds. I'm my own person. She's her own person. I can't go along with her childish game forever. Even if I wanted to, everybody has to go home eventually. And if you look a year or ten years into the future, that's an undeniable fact.

"How long are you going to keep grumbling? Shouldn't you already be used to being seen in this outfit?"

I could see Haruhi dragging Asahina away from the trees.

"Behave like an actress. Bravely shedding your clothes is the fast track to a blue-ribbon rookie award! Not that you'll be shedding your clothes this time. Have to keep something in reserve."

She looked like a hunting hound bringing in a rabbit. Haruhi returned with bunny-girl Asahina, wearing high heels that didn't look very suitable for walking on the dirt. She had a smile so bright, I was expecting her to sneeze at any moment.

"Once this movie's a success, I'll use the proceeds to take everyone to a hot spring. Think of it as a vacation. Mikuru wants to go, right?"

Still . . . Well, whatever. I'll follow this through to the end. I would have preferred to be involved in something like the story from your movie. It would have been perfect if I were in the Itsuki Koizumi character's position, but it appears that I don't have any hidden powers.

I'll just behave and play your straight man.

In a few years, we'll all be able to look back and go, "Yeah, we did some crazy stuff back then," and laugh about all of this.

Probably.

Bunny-girl Asahina walked along, looking even more embarrassed than when she was a waitress. Haruhi was the only one who had a smug look on her face. What are you so happy about?

I pretended to fiddle with the focus on the video camera as I zoomed in on Asahina's cleavage. You know, I have to check that thing.

A small mole rested on her white, left mound. Upon closer inspection, it was shaped like a star. Confirmation complete. This person's definitely my Asahina. Not a fake.

"What are you doing?"

Haruhi's face popped up in front of the lens.

"You're not allowed to shoot anything I didn't order. We're not filming your home videos."

I know. Notice how I haven't pressed the record button. I was just looking.

"Okay, everybody, gather around! And get ready! We'll be shooting Mikuru's daily life now. Mikuru, you just walk around naturally. And the camera will follow."

"What kind of girl shows up at a forest park in a bunny-girl outfit on a daily basis?"

"Who cares about that? It's considered normal in the movie. Trying to apply realistic standards to fiction is just weird."

I'd like to return that line straight back at you. Except that in your case, you're applying fictional standards to reality so it's the other way around.

Afterward, Asahina, unaware that she could fire killer beams from her eyes, plucked flowers from the park, gathered dead leaves and blew them into the air, and danced and hopped around on the grass per Haruhi's instructions, growing more and more exhausted in the process.

And then Haruhi dealt the final blow.

"Hmm. Doesn't feel right with mountains in the background. I suppose a bunny girl wouldn't be walking around the mountains. Let's head into town!"

With that complete reversal of what she'd been saying just a moment prior, we found ourselves on the bus and on the move again.

The leading actor, Koizumi, who at this point had been on lighting duty the whole time, was holding on to the strap with the taped-up reflector board and other items I had forced on him tucked under his arm.

I was standing next to him, and Nagato stood next to me, like a dark shadow. Only Haruhi and Asahina were sitting in the empty seats. Haruhi had taken the camera from me and sat right next to Asahina, filming her from the side.

Asahina had her head down as she answered Haruhi's questions in a subdued voice. It looked like the director was conducting an interview of the lead actress.

The bus traveled down the winding mountain road toward the residential area. I prayed earnestly inside my heart that the driver wasn't constantly looking in the rearview mirror. Please drive with your eyes looking forward.

Perhaps my prayers were heard, since our bus safely reached the station, our destination. By this point, the bus was filled with passengers who were all staring at Haruhi, Asahina, and Nagato. The sight of those bouncy bunny ears and her exposed creamy shoulders and back was devastating. It felt like the bunny version of Asahina would be the talk of not only North High, but the entire city.

That might be Haruhi's aim. "There was a pretty bunny girl on the bus yesterday." "Yeah, I saw her too." "What's that you say?" "I think she belongs to North High's SOS Brigade." "SOS Brigade?" "Yes, the SOS Brigade." "The SOS Brigade, huh? I'll remember that." That's probably how she expects it to go. Asahina isn't the SOS Brigade's billboard. So what is she? you might ask. Obviously, she serves as the tea girl and my spiritual balm. I'm sure that's what Asahina wants. Definitely.

Of course, trying to tell Haruhi what you want is like trying to talk to a wall. Thanks to Haruhi's miraculous mechanism that repels anything inconvenient anyone else might have to say away from her eardrums. It might be osmotic pressure. If I figure out how it works, the Nobel Prize committee might at least consider me a nominee in the Physiology category. Anybody want to give it a shot? (The trick is to just casually throw it out there.)

That day, Asahina was stuck as a bunny girl until the sun set. As for what she did, well, she just walked around in that outfit. This wasn't much different from the usual magical mystery patrol, except that the extra attention just made it all the more tiring and I was constantly worrying if someone might call the cops. Haruhi had no concept of what "approval to film" was, so she was free to shoot wherever she wanted. Her sense of freedom was about as dignified as papal authority during the age of Innocent III — I would say. Her definition of "freedom" was mistaken.

"That's enough for today."

Haruhi finally had a look on her face signaling that our work was done, and the rest of us, except for Nagato, breathed a sigh of relief. It had been a long day. Tomorrow's Sunday and I want a long, hard rest.

"Okay, see everybody tomorrow then. Meet up at the same time and place as today," she said as though it were no big deal. We'll be receiving compensatory time, right?

"What's that? You realize that we're behind in filming? There isn't time for people to be relaxing! You can rest all you want once the cultural festival is over. Until we're finished, assume that red-letter days don't exist on the calendar!"

We're already behind schedule after two days of filming. Can you work on your time-management skills? Behind? Does that mean the hours of footage I shot today aren't going to be used? Or does Haruhi intend to make a Taiga drama? We're not making a daily broadcast show here. Just a one-shot amateur movie to screen at a cultural festival.

In any case, Haruhi didn't look like she was worried about a single thing. She shoved all the equipment on me and, carrying only her armband and cell phone, turned with a top-class smile on her face.

"See you all tomorrow then! We're definitely going to make this movie a success. No, with my directorial vision, the movie is already guaranteed to be a success. The rest depends on how hard you people work. Make sure you show up on time. If anyone doesn't show up, there will be lynching and heads will roll!"

And with that proclamation, she walked off humming Marilyn Manson's "Rock Is Dead."

"I'll let Asahina know," Koizumi whispered in my ear before he left. Asahina had Koizumi's blazer draped over her head. If it were winter, I'd have brought a coat, but unfortunately the weather had been stuck in a late-summer pattern. I directed an irritated glare at the pile of items next to my feet.

"Let her know what?"

"About the laser we were discussing. There shouldn't be any odd rays being fired if her eye doesn't change color. That's how it works according to Suzumiya's rules, so we should be okay if she doesn't put on any color contacts."

The reflector-board-carrying leading bastard flashed me what looked like one of those insurance-salesman smiles.

"Let us err on the side of caution and prepare a safety net. I'm sure she will be willing to cooperate. After all, beams are dangerous."

Koizumi walked over to the black-garbed figure that looked something like a human crow, Nagato.

As I returned home carrying my huge load of crap, my sister came out to greet me, looking at me like I was some kind of weird animal. The grade-schooler who had been responsible for the nickname "Kyon" spreading all over started spouting stuff like "Is that a video camera? Yay, film me, film me!" and other nonsense, but I just said "Moron" and went to my room.

In any case, I was completely exhausted. Any desire to engage in any further unbecoming cameraman activities had long evaporated. Asahina was one thing, but why should I have to engage in something as sad as recording footage of my own little sister? No fun in that.

I set down my bag along with the backpack and paper bags before collapsing on my bed, attaining a brief moment's respite before my mother sent my sister up to elbow-smash me awake for dinner.

CHAPTER 4

The next day, we gathered in front of the station yet again. The only difference would be that there had been a switch in members. In addition to the SOS Brigade members, there were three new faces standing before me. They were the underling characters Haruhi had mentioned.

"Hey, Kyon. This isn't how you said it would be."

Taniguchi was filing some sort of protest.

"Where's the lovely Asahina? I only came 'cause you said she'd be here to greet us. She's not here, chief."

Exactly. The scheduled time had passed and Asahina still hadn't shown up. She's most likely cooped up inside her room, refusing to go outside, considering how much she went through yesterday and the day before.

"I came here for the eye candy. And what's this? All I've seen so far is Suzumiya's pissed-off face. This is a scam."

Shut up. Why don't you look at Nagato or something?

"In any case, that outfit really suits Nagato," Kunikida commented in a carefree tone. He would be the second underling after

Taniguchi. The night before, I had just gotten into the bathtub when Haruhi called. I took the phone from my sister and answered it as I washed my hair.

"That moron Taniguchi and the other one . . . I can't remember his name, but anyway, your friend. Bring the two of them with you tomorrow. We'll be using them for underlings."

And with that she hung up. Didn't even say hello. When you ask people to do something for you, you should try sounding more appealing — the way Asahina sounds — instead of just barking out orders.

Once I was done with my bath, I called Taniguchi and Kunikida to ask if they had any plans for the weekend, and the bored side duo immediately consented to come. What do you guys usually do on the weekend?

Maybe Haruhi thought that two guys by themselves wouldn't make for much of a shot, but whatever the case, she had prepared another extra. That person was currently bent over, peering into Nagato's face under her wide-brimmed hat. With a toss of her long hair, she stood straight and turned to greet me with a smile.

"Kyon, what happened to Mikuru?"

The cheerful girl was Tsuruya, Asahina's classmate. According to Asahina, she was "a friend from this time period," so I would assume she doesn't have a weird background. Back in June when Haruhi was like "Let's enter a baseball tournament" and we needed more people, Asahina brought this normal second-year female high-schooler. Oh yeah, Taniguchi and Kunikida were also around for that one. My sister too, while we're at it.

Tsuruya bared her healthy white teeth for all to see.

"So, what're we doing? I was told to come if I happened to be free. What's it say on Suzumiya's armband? Whatcha gonna do with that video camera? Why's Yuki dressed like that?"

She fired the stream of questions in rapid succession. By the time I had opened my mouth to respond, Tsuruya had already moved on to Koizumi.

"Whoa, Koizumi! Looking sharp today."

Busy person.

Still, Haruhi could give Tsuruya a run for her money when it comes to hyperactivity. Pretty impressive how she could yell at her cell phone so loudly this early in the morning.

"What are you talking about? You're the star! Thirty percent of this movie's success is riding on you! Though the other seventy percent depends on my talent. Whatever! What was that? Your stomach hurts? Stupid! That excuse is only going to work in grade school! Get your ass down here right now! Within thirty seconds!"

It would appear that Asahina's suffering from an onset of hikikomori syndrome. It was inevitable. Wouldn't be the least bit surprised if the mere thought of having to endure yet another day of torture would be enough to emotionally induce stomach pains. Since she's a timid person.

"Sheesh!"

Haruhi hung up in a rage with a look on her face like a butler about to scold a child for not using proper table manners.

"She needs to be punished!"

Don't be like that. Asahina, unlike you, just wants to live a quiet life. You could leave her in peace on Sunday, at least, that's what I think.

Of course, Haruhi wasn't going to listen to any selfish requests from her leading actress. This female director kept a short leash on her star, even when she wasn't paying her a penny.

"I'll go pick her up. Hand me that bag over there."

She snatched a clear bag containing the costumes and sprinted off to the taxi stand. She then pounded on the window of a

parked taxi until the door was opened, before jumping in and riding off somewhere.

That's right. I don't know where Asahina lives. Though I've been to Nagato's place a number of times. . . .

"I can understand how Asahina feels."

Koizumi had moved to stand next to me when I wasn't paying attention. Tsuruya was with the joker combo from my class saying stuff like "Hey, it's been a while" as they bowed and fawned over her. Koizumi smiled as he watched them.

"After all, there's an impression that she may actually become a real transforming heroine at this rate. Anyway, the laser rays were definitely over the top."

"What wouldn't be over the top?"

"Let's see. Something on the level of breathing fire from her mouth would be simple to set up."

"Asahina isn't supposed to be a monster, performer, or evil wrestler. What if her lovely lips get burned? Nobody could possibly shoulder the responsibility for that. Don't tell me you're already planning on taking responsibility for her."

"Not at all. The only time I would ever feel responsibility would be if I were to allow the Celestials to run wild. Fortunately, that has never happened . . . ah, it happened once, didn't it? I must thank you for your actions during that time. Your help allowed us to get through the incident."

Half a year ago, the world had been on the verge of being destroyed. Thanks to excruciating physical effort and exhausting mental exertion on my part, the world was able to hang on by a thread. I figured it wouldn't be odd to expect world leaders to send me thank-you letters, but I have yet to hear from any embassy staff. Well, it'd be a problem if they actually did show up, so I'm not really hoping for anything. I received a reward last time in the form of an embrace from a sobbing Asahina, and when I thought about it, that was more than enough. It wasn't like Koizumi saying thanks was going to make me happy.

"About Mikuru Asahina . . ."

"Don't use her first name. It gives me an unpleasant feeling."

"Excuse me. About Asahina, it appears that we will be able to avoid having her emit odd rays."

"How'd you manage that? Are you just being really optimistic and assuming that Haruhi didn't prepare a spare color contact?"

"No, it's already been taken care of. Nagato was very cooperative."

I looked over at the unmoving girl staring at shops in front of the station before looking back at Koizumi. "What'd you do to Asahina?"

"There's no need to look angry. We merely eliminated any exposure to laser. I don't entirely understand it myself. Nagato, unlike the other TFEI terminals, speaks very little. I simply requested for her to remove any risk of danger."

"What's TFEI?"

"An abbreviation we arbitrarily assigned. It's not exactly vital information. However, I believe that Nagato stands out, even when compared with the rest of them. I believe that she may serve another purpose beyond a mere interface."

What else would the tight-mouthed bookworm do besides observe Haruhi? Ryoko Asakura would be missed by more people. Not that I miss her, though.

After thirty minutes, the taxi Haruhi had taken returned. Waitress Asahina was in tow, looking as glum as she did yesterday. Haruhi was getting a receipt from the driver. Maybe she intended to write off the taxi fee as an expense.

Taniguchi and Kunikida were holding some kind of discussion as they watched.

"The other night, I'd gone to the convenience store and was on my way back when I passed a taxi."

"Huh."

"And then I noticed that the *Taxi* sign on the roof looked like it said *Love.*"

"Wowzers."

"But the taxi sped off before I could get another look. That's when I realized. Love is what I'm missing right now."

"Maybe it really did say *Love.* It must have been a private taxi."

To think that we have to ask two idiots engaged in such a ridiculous conversation for help. We must really be scraping the bottom of the personnel barrel. If I were to compare Taniguchi and Kunikida to nickel alloy, then Tsuruya would be platinum. They're about as different as fireworks and Apollo 11.

"Hey, hey. Mikuru, who do you think you are to come by taxi?"

Tsuruya was pretty psyched up, but it was at a mild level. Nowhere near Haruhi's crazy natural high. You could say that Tsuruya was still grounded within the realm of the normal world.

"Wow, amazing! Sexy! Mikuru, what's the place you're working at? Must not allow anyone under eighteen inside. Huh? Aren't you only seventeen? Oh, right. You're not a customer so it's okay."

Asahina's eyes, puffy from crying, were their natural color. Looks like they're out of color contacts.

Haruhi dragged the petite waitress out front.

"You're not going to get away with pretending to be sick! We're going to keep on filming! Mikuru, this will be your time to shine. Everything is for the SOS Brigade! The spirit of self-sacrifice will always move the audience, no matter what world you live in!"

You be the sacrifice.

"There can only be one heroine in this world. It really should be me, but I'm giving up the seat this time as a special service. At least, until the cultural festival's over!"

Nobody in this world accepts you as the heroine.

Tsuruya was slapping Asahina on the shoulder as she talked.

"What's this? Race queen? Some kind of character? Oh, that's it. Let's use this for the yakisoba café at the cultural festival! A bunch of customers will come!"

I can understand why Asahina wanted to coop herself up in her room. No pitcher's going to stand on the mound when he knows a rally is about to start.

Asahina slowly raised her head and looked at me with the eyes of a martyr, begging for salvation, before quickly looking away. She let loose a soft sigh before offering a wan smile and dragging her feet over to me.

"Sorry I'm late."

I was looking at the top of Asahina's head as she bowed down.

"Nah, I don't really mind."

"I guess I'll have to pay for everyone's lunch. . . ."

"No way, don't sweat it."

"I'm sorry about yesterday. It looks like I fired some kind optical weapon without realizing it. . . ."

"No sweat, I was perfectly fine. . . ."

I took a quick peek. Nagato was standing around absentmindedly with the star-tipped antenna in her hand. Noticing my reaction, Asahina lowered her already soft and fine voice.

"I was bitten."

She rubbed her left wrist.

"Bitten by what?"

"Nagato. She said something about injecting nanomachines. . . . But it looks like my eyes will no longer emit anything. What a relief."

Which means I don't have to worry about getting sliced up, huh? Still, it's hard to picture Nagato biting Asahina. So, what exactly did she inject?

"It was last night. She came with Koizumi to my home. . . ."

Koizumi, in charge of keeping an eye on the equipment, was talking with Haruhi about something. I would have loved to have come along. Invite me to these kinds of things. I'd much rather be invited on a visit to Asahina's home instead of closed space.

"Whatcha whispering about?"

Tsuruya wrapped her flexible arm around Asahina's neck.

"Mikuru sure is cute. I'd love to keep her at my place. Kyon, are you guys getting along?"

Absolutely.

Taniguchi and Kunikida, the hack combo, were admiring Asahina, who had her mouth half open. Don't stare. What if you damage her looks? That was when Haruhi shouted.

"We've decided on a place!"

"For what?"

"Filming."

Oh, yeah. I'd almost forgotten that we were shooting a movie here. Actually, I want to forget. It feels more like we're producing a cheap idol DVD, oddly enough.

"There's a large pond near Koizumi's house. We'll start filming there today!"

Haruhi was already out in front, carrying a vinyl flag with the words *Film Crew* written on it and leading the way.

I called over Taniguchi and Kunikida, who were still staring inappropriately at Asahina, and we shared the bags and packs among us.

* * *

After thirty minutes of walking, we reached the bank of the pond. It was located within some hills in approximately the center of the residential district. It was pretty big for a pond. Big enough for migratory birds to drop by during winter, and according to Koizumi, it was the time of year when ducks and geese started showing up.

There was a metal fence surrounding the pond area, barring entry. There was an issue of common sense first, though. Or maybe a problem with how kids are being raised. Either way, you're not going to find grade-schoolers playing around in a place like this these days, unless they're really dumb.

"What are you doing? Hurry up and jump over."

I'd forgotten that this girl was, in fact, really dumb. Haruhi the director had her foot on the fence and was beckoning to the rest of us. Asahina had a look of despair on her face as she held down her short skirt. Tsuruya was cackling next to her.

"What? What are we doing here? Wa-ha-ha! Is Mikuru going to swim?"

With a shake of her head, Asahina eyed the green surface as though if it were a lake of blood. Sigh.

"The fence is a tad high to climb. Don't you agree?"

Koizumi was talking to Nagato, not me. It was pretty futile to try to hold a conversation with her. She either gave you a simple yes or no or went into a long spiel nobody could understand.

"..."

However, while Nagato remained silent, she showed a curious reaction. She put her fingers on a metal pole supporting the fence and pulled it to the side. What was supposed to be an iron pole bent as easily as caramel under a burning sun, and eventually came to a rest in a bent state.

As skillful as always. I quickly turned to look at the other people, though it was probably unnecessary.

"Huh, it must be old," Kunikida said with a knowledgeable look on his face.

"So what am I supposed to do? Am I a kappa?" Taniguchi muttered to himself as he squeezed through an opening in the fence and headed to the bank of the pond.

"I live in the area. There didn't used to be a fence here. I spent a lot of time here."

Tsuruya followed, leading Asahina by the hand, looking very reluctant, toward the edge of the pond where Haruhi was waiting.

The three extras weren't concerning themselves with any small details. That's a big help.

Koizumi smiled equally at both Nagato and me before he slipped through the fence. Nagato, looking like a black mage, passed in front of me like a ghost.

Not like I have a choice. I just have to get this filming over with and get out of here. Before anybody starts asking any questions about destruction of public property.

Asahina and Nagato stood facing each other again. Looks like another battle scene. Is Haruhi actually trying to come up with a story here? When is Koizumi going to make an appearance? Koizumi, in his uniform, was once again standing behind me on lighting duty.

After placing her director's chair on the muddy ground, Haruhi began furiously scribbling what I would assume was the dialogue in a sketchbook.

"In this scene, Mikuru finally finds herself in a dire situation. Because her blue eye beam has been sealed by Yuki."

The felt pen came to a halt as she looked up with a self-satisfied look on her face.

"Yeah, that sounds good. You there. Hold this up while standing."

And just like that, Taniguchi was on cue-card duty. The two actresses looked to the hands of the sulking Taniguchi.

"Th-th-this won't be enough to discourage me! E-e-evil alien Yuki! Quietly leave Earth at once . . . Um . . . I'm sorry."

In response to Mikuru Asahina's unexpected apology, the evil alien mage Yuki Nagato opened her mouth.

". . . I see."

She nodded without any sign that she had taken offense. She then read her lines in a deadpan voice per Haruhi's instructions.

"You should be the one to vanish from this time. He will fall into our hands. That is how much he is worth. He has yet to realize his own power, but it is a valuable thing. Consequently, we will start by invading Earth."

Haruhi waved her megaphone around like a conductor, and Nagato pointed the star-tipped antenna at Asahina's face in a similar motion.

"I-I-I won't let you have your way! Even if it costs me my life!"

"Then we shall take your life."

Asahina shook noticeably in response to Nagato's flat words.

"Cut!" yelled Haruhi as she stood up. She ran over between the two of them.

"You're starting to get the feel of it. Yep, that's the spirit. But no ad-libbing, okay? And Mikuru, come over here."

The director and leading actress turned their backs on the rest of us. I lowered the video camera and stretched out my neck. I wondered what they were discussing.

After about a second, Tsuruya was no longer able to hold herself back and began cackling in a loud voice.

"What's this movie about? Or is it even a movie? Wa-ha-ha. It's absolutely hysterical!"

Except the only other person able to enjoy this movie besides you would be Haruhi.

Taniguchi and Kunikida were lounging around with looks on their faces that said, *Why were we called here?* Nagato was playing dumb by herself. Koizumi was gazing across the pond as though he'd become one with nature. I removed the almost-filled tape and unwrapped a new DV cassette. It felt like I was just creating more garbage.

Tsuruya was looking at my hands with great interest.

"Hmm. This is what videos look like these days? A bunch of Mikuru pictures are on here? Can you show me later? It'll probably be great for laughs."

It's not a laughing matter. Passing out flyers in a bunny-girl outfit had been a one-day affair, but this stupid filming could potentially go on until the day before the cultural festival. Asahina could go from refusing to stand in front of a camera to refusing to go to school. That would hurt me the hardest. Since I would no longer be able to drink her marvelous tea. Nagato's tea has no taste, and Haruhi's is bad on a fundamental level. Koizumi's is out of the question. If I end up in a situation where I have to make my own tea, I'd rather drink tap water.

"Sorry for the wait!"

Yeah, you kept us waiting. Waiting and waiting. About time to go home, I'd say. We wouldn't want to trample too much pond-side foliage.

"We're just getting to the good stuff. Here, look at this!"

Haruhi shoved Asahina out in front with a push. Look, you say? Don't need you to tell me that. I stare at her every day. See, it's the usual, same beautiful, adorable, and fair Asahina . . .

"Ah?"

One of her eyes was a different color. The right eye this time. A silver eye looked apologetically between the ground and me.

"Come on, Mikuru. Use that Miracle Mikuru Eye-R to fire something, anything fantastic, and attack!"

I didn't even have time to tell her to stop. Even if there had been enough time, I would still have gotten sliced and diced. At any rate, it was all too sudden. Haruhi delivering the dangerous command, Asahina blinking in surprise, and also —

The dark figure of Nagato pushing down Asahina by the pond.

A re-creation of the scene from yesterday. It was like watching a replay. Nagato had used her special teleportation again.

In an instant only her hat remained where she had been standing, and it softly floated to the ground. The person who had been wearing that hat had, in the blink of an eye (probably around 0.2 seconds), traveled a number of meters to ride Asahina. Iron claw to the temples.

Everyone watched dumbfounded as the two actresses began wrestling on the damp ground.

"Na-Na-Nagato . . . Hee!"

The wordless and expressionless Nagato paid her screaming no heed and straddled Asahina with just a slight ruffle of her short hair.

"Hey!" Haruhi quickly recovered.

"Yuki! You're a mage! You're supposed to be bad at physical combat! This isn't the time to be mud wrestling —"

However, Haruhi shut her mouth mid-sentence and spent three seconds thinking.

"Well, this works too. Since it'll probably sell. Kyon! Make sure you're filming! Let's not waste Yuki's idea."

This isn't by design. She's reacting to the situation. Some kind of defensive measure to deal with the contact lens. I'm sure Asahina understands that, but she's so scared that all she can do is cry out softly and kick her legs. Tantalizing. No, I mean, now's not the time to be aiming for a fan-service shot.

That was when a rattle made everyone besides those two look behind us.

The fence around the pond that Haruhi had climbed and the rest of us had squeezed through. The space it had occupied was now empty. The fence, cut in a V-shape, was now lying on the road, as though it had been hit by an invisible laser.

After a moment, I looked back to find Nagato biting into Asahina's wrist like an anemic vampire.

"I was careless."

Surprisingly, Nagato was criticizing herself.

"The laser was configured to disperse and become harmless. This time, it was a hyper-oscillatory particle cutter," she murmured in a tone that suggested she wasn't breathing.

Koizumi, picking up the black hat and offering it to her, opened his mouth. "Something like monofilament, I presume. But if the particle cutter isn't visible to the eye, it must have no mass?"

Nagato took the hat and casually put it on her head.

"I perceived a trace amount of mass. Approximately equivalent to one over ten to the forty-first power grams."

"Less than a neutrino?"

Nagato remained silent as she stared into Asahina's eyes. The waitress's right eye was still silver.

"Um . . ."

Asahina wiggled around as she rubbed her bitten wrist.

"What did you, um, inject into me this, this time . . . ?"

The tip of the pointy hat moved about five millimeters. I took that as a sign of confusion. She must have been fretting over how to word her response. And just as expected, Nagato responded.

"A force field was established on the surface with the ability to phase-shift dimensional oscillatory cycles and transform them into gravitational waves."

She delivered that baffling sentence in a strained voice. I had no idea how that would eliminate the killer wire, but for some reason beyond my comprehension the other two people appeared to accept the explanation. Koizumi was saying irrelevant things like "I see. Incidentally, gravity manifests itself in waves?" Nagato probably also thought his question was irrelevant. Since she didn't give him an answer.

Koizumi shrugged like it was some kind of signature pose.

"However, we certainly were careless. This was also my responsibility. I was only expecting laser beams to shoot from her eyes. *Fire something, anything fantastic,* were her words I believe. It seems other people aren't allowed to follow Suzumiya's train of thought. She's an amazing person."

Follow her train of thought? More like she's already lapped the rest of humanity multiple times. A whole three laps even. And you can feel the pressure as she creeps up from behind. It's so intense that at first glance, a person in the stands might be confused and assume you were on the same lap. That's something only people racing on the circuit would know, and Haruhi isn't going to ease on the pedal, be it an S-curve, a Degner curve, or a crisscrossing one. And on top of all that, she's the only one with a Bussard ramjet engine, which allows her keep going forever. She's set up the rules so that nobody could keep up with her, even if they wanted to. And she has no idea that this whole thing is fixed. When matters are this serious, you can't just laugh it all off because she happens to be clueless.

"Well, fortunately," said Koizumi, "everyone appears to have accepted that the fence had deteriorated due to poor maintenance by the local government. I'm glad the matter didn't get out of hand."

I glanced at the pale face hidden under the hat. Yuki'd shown us her palm, which looked like it'd been sliced up by a whirlwind. A picture gruesome enough to scare people who can't stand pain. Except it was healing so fast, it was as if it'd never happened.

I looked over at the second group, standing some distance away. Haruhi and the haphazard trio of extras were watching the video on the camera and shouting in a melodic voice . . . or that was just Tsuruya.

"What do we do?" I asked. "I feel like there's going to be a disaster if we keep filming."

"However, we cannot simply call off the movie," Koizumi replied. "What do you think will happen if we force Suzumiya to stop filming this movie?"

"She'll probably go berserk."

"Most assuredly. Even if she didn't personally go around wreaking havoc, we can rest assured that Celestials would be rampaging within closed space."

Don't remind me. I never want to go there again. I never want to do that again.

"Most likely, Suzumiya is having too much fun in the current situation. She's able to freely engage her imagination and create her own movie. Almost like playing God. As you already know, she is usually irritated by how reality doesn't work the way she desires. That's actually not true, but since she hasn't realized it, the result is the same. However, in this movie, the story progresses according to her wishes. Anything is possible. Suzumiya is using this movie as a medium to reconstruct a world."

She's as selfish as ever. You can't have what you want unless you're extremely rich or powerful. Go become a politician or something.

As my face cycled through a variety of grimaces and frowns, Koizumi continued talking with a smile on his face.

"Of course, Suzumiya is not aware of that. She believes that she is creating a fictional world within the movie. Her earnest passion is focused on the production of this film. I would presume that her passion is so great that she's unconsciously affected the real world.

"It's like rolling a die that only has negative numbers on it. We can't just continue filming and let Haruhi's delusions run wild. We can't stop filming and put her in a bad mood. Both choices lead straight to bad endings.

"Nonetheless, if we must choose between the two, I would prefer to continue."

"Give me a good reason why," I asked.

"I've grown tired of hunting Celestials. . . . I'm just kidding. Sorry about that. Let's see, the reason is basically as follows. Allowing a few alterations to the world would appear more conducive to our survival than letting the entire world be reset."

So we just allow Asahina to become Superwoman in the real world?

"This time, the alterations to reality are quite modest when compared with Celestials. After all, Nagato is able to effectively utilize protective revisions. When compared with the prospect of starting the world over from scratch, wouldn't you agree that dealing with supernormal phenomena case by case sounds vastly preferable?"

"I'd have to say that neither scenario sounds very good. What if we whack Haruhi from behind and knock her out until the cultural festival's over?"

"What a frightful notion. But if you take full responsibility, I won't stop you."

"I can't shoulder the entire world."

And with that reply, I turned to look at Asahina, who was picking dirt off the waitress costume with her fingers. She looked like she'd pretty much given up hope. Upon noticing my gaze, she quickly opened her mouth.

"D-don't worry about me. I'll get through this somehow. . . ."

So sweet. Her face looks pretty pale, though. Well yeah, I'm pretty sure she doesn't want to be bitten by Nagato every time something comes up. Even if the tooth marks do disappear shortly, it doesn't change the fact that it's creepy. After all, if I were to give Nagato a long-handled sickle, she'd look like Death-girl from the thirteenth tarot card or an ageless space vampire. Either way, she's going to be sending you to the beyond.

Of course, in Asahina's case, it was injecting instead of sucking. Still, even if you attribute this all to carelessness, Asahina seems to have a weak sense of danger for someone from the future. Maybe it's because I don't know how she really feels. Since it involves a bunch of classified information.

Well, I'm sure she'll tell me one of these days. And of course, we should all be alone in a confined space when it happens.

It was finally time for Taniguchi and Kunikida, along with Tsuruya.

When Haruhi revealed their roles in the movie, we learned that they would play nameless bit characters. Their roles were listed as "Normal people being manipulated as slave puppets by evil alien Yuki."

"In other words," Haruhi explained with an unpleasant grin on her face, "Mikuru fights for justice so she can't harm normal people. Yuki is taking advantage of that weakness. She's using hypnotic magic to control normal humans. Mikuru, unable to fight against ordinary civilians, gets all beat up."

Asahina's pretty beaten up already. What more do you intend to do to her? By the time I finished that thought, Haruhi was already talking again.

"Start by throwing Mikuru into the pond."

"What!"

Asahina was the only one reacting with surprise. Tsuruya was guffawing to the side. Taniguchi and Kunikida looked at each other before turning to Asahina's bewildered face.

"Hey, now," Taniguchi said with a strange half smile on his face. "The pond? The water might be warm, but it's fall already. Even the most generous fool in the world wouldn't call this water clean."

"Su-Su-Suzumiya, at least use a warm-water pool. . . ."

Asahina was presenting her earnest objection, on the verge of tears. Even Kunikida was defending her.

"That's right. What if it's a bottomless bog? She'll never float back up again. Look, there's a bunch of black bass."

Don't say stuff that'll make Asahina faint. Also, it's already been proven that the more you resist, the more stubborn Haruhi gets. True to form, her lips were puckered like a duck's bill.

"Shut up. Okay? Sacrifices must be made for the sake of realism. I wanted to use Loch Ness or the Great Salt Lake for this scene. But we don't have the time or money for that. It is our duty as humans to do the best we can in the limited time we are given. Which means we have to use this pond."

What kind of logic is that? And this conversation seems to assume that Asahina has to suffer water torture. You could just switch the background you know. Why can't you use your mind that way?

As I was pondering whether I should stop her, someone tapped my shoulder from behind. I turned back to see damn Koizumi with a thin smile on his face, wordlessly shaking his head. I know. Tamper with Haruhi the wrong way and weird stuff will start happening. If Asahina starts shooting plasma fireballs from her mouth, we might have the Japan Self-Defense Forces coming after us.

"Ah, I'll do it!" Asahina announced in a bitter voice.

She must be heartbroken. Here's a poor girl sacrificing herself for world peace. An incredibly cliché development that would probably be the climax of the making-of video. Except the camera isn't rolling.

Haruhi was simply thrilled.

"Mikuru, that's great! You look divine right now! That's what I would expect from one of my handpicked brigade members! You've really grown!"

It's more like she's learned rather than grown, I'd say.

"Then the two of you each take one of Mikuru's arms, and Tsuru can hold her legs. When I say ready, go. Once I've said it, toss her into the pond."

The following scene played out under Haruhi's direction.

The three extras started by standing in a line in front of Nagato with their heads hanging as the black-garbed mage waved the antenna pointer. It almost looked like some kind of Shinto exorcism ceremony. As I watched Nagato's blank face while she moved the pointer, she did have a sort of shrine-maiden feel to her.

Afterward, having received Nagato's command to target Asahina, the three of them moved toward the heroine, walking stiffly like zombies seeking fresh meat.

"Mikuru! Sorry. I really don't want to do this, but I'm being mind-controlled and stuff. Really, I'm sorry."

Tsuruya, who looked like she was having the absolute time of her life, crept toward the waitress with a smile reminiscent of a cat-shaped bus. Taniguchi, always timid in a pinch, pretended to hesitate while Kunikida scratched at his head as they both approached Asahina, who turned pale, then red.

"Hey, you two morons! Be serious about this!"

You're the moron. But I swallowed that comment and continued looking through the camera. Asahina, knees buckling, slowly backed up to the edge of the pond.

"Prepare yourself!" Tsuruya said brightly as she shoved Asahina down and hoisted an exposed thigh under each arm. What should I say? This is getting dangerous.

"He . . . hee!"

Asahina was seriously scared. Taniguchi and Kunikida each grabbed an arm.

"W-w-wait, actually I . . . i-i-is this really necessary?"

Paying no heed to Asahina's painful cries, Haruhi nodded solemnly.

"It's to make this scene better, in other words, for the sake of art!"

A common expression, but I have to wonder where the art is in this half-assed amateur film.

Haruhi barked the order.

"Now! Ready, go!"

Splash. A large amount of water sprayed out as the aquatic inhabitants of the pond had their lives disturbed.

"Ah, hel . . . wah . . . !"

Really good job of acting like you're drowning, Asahina . . . or I'm getting a feeling that she's really drowning. Who knows.

"My feet . . . won't reach . . . Ah!"

Good thing we weren't in the Amazon region. If she were splashing around like this down there, she'd make an easy target for the piranhas. I wondered if black bass attacked people — as I looked through the viewfinder, when I discovered that Asahina wasn't the only one splashing around.

"Crap! I swallowed water!"

Taniguchi was drowning. Apparently, the momentum from throwing Asahina had carried him into the water. We didn't need to worry about him.

"What's that idiot doing?"

Haruhi apparently agreed and ignored the moron as she pointed the megaphone at Koizumi.

"Okay, Koizumi. It's your turn! Go save Mikuru."

The leading actor, who had been stuck on lighting duty, smiled elegantly as he handed the reflector board to Nagato and ran over to the edge of the pond, extending his hand.

"Please grab on. Calm down. Try not to drag me in as well."

Asahina clung to Koizumi's arm like a shipwreck victim clinging to a piece of driftwood. Koizumi gently lifted the soaked time-traveling combat waitress and held her close to his body. Hey, that's too close.

"Are you all right?"

". . . Ugh . . . it was cold . . ."

Her already tight costume, now soaked, was practically transparent. If I were a member of the Motion Picture Code of Ethics Committee, I would ban anyone under fifteen from watching this movie without any hesitation. To be honest, this feels worse than full nudity. It feels like we might get arrested.

"Yep, perfect!"

Haruhi was whacking the megaphone as she shouted triumphantly. I ignored Taniguchi, still splashing away in the pond, and hit the stop button on the video camera.

* * *

We had enough crap to open up a vending stall, yet we didn't have a single towel?

Asahina's eyes remained shut tight as she wiped her face with Tsuruya's handkerchief. I stood next to Haruhi, breathing silently, as she diligently checked the video.

"Yeah, not bad."

Haruhi nodded after playing back Asahina's drowning scene three times.

"The scene of their meeting was adequate. You can feel how Itsuki and Mikuru are still awkward around each other at this point. Yep, yep."

Really? Koizumi looked the same as always.

"The second step is next. Itsuki, after saving Mikuru, decides to hide her in his own home. That's where the next scene will start."

"Er, wait. That doesn't flow at all. Where did Nagato, the one controlling Taniguchi and the others, go off to? And Team Taniguchi, what about them? How were they stopped? Even underlings need a proper portrayal or the audience isn't going buy it."

"You sure are annoying. People will understand what happened without us filming it. You can just skip the boring parts!"

Freak. You just wanted to throw Asahina into the pond, huh?

As I grew enraged, Tsuruya raised her hand and spoke.

"Heya. My house is close by. Mikuru looks like she's about to catch a cold so can I get her a change of clothes?"

"That's perfect!" Haruhi cried as her shining eyes focused on Tsuruya.

"Can we borrow your room, Tsuruya? I want to film Itsuki and Mikuru getting friendly there. What a smooth turn of events. This movie will definitely be a success!"

For Haruhi, whose main theme in life is apparently opportunism, that's probably a convenient proposal, yeah. I can't get rid of the gnawing suspicion that Tsuruya only brought it up because Haruhi wished it to be so. Except that Haruhi accepted Tsuruya as an underling, so she should be just as ordinary as me.

"Uh, what about us?"

Kunikida raised that question. Taniguchi stood next to him wringing out his shirt.

"You guys can go home," Haruhi said heartlessly. "Good work. Bye, so long. We may never meet again."

The names of those two classmates must have been erased from Haruhi's mind at that point. Without another look at Kunikida, with a shocked look on his face, or Taniguchi, shaking water from his hair like a dog, Haruhi dubbed Tsuruya our guide and walked off. Lucky for you guys. Your job is done. Apparently, you're worth as much as expended BBs as far as Haruhi's concerned. That's actually something to be happy about.

Tsuruya was also pumped up for some reason as she talked happily.

"Okay. Everybody, it's this way!"

She stood at the head waving the flag around.

It's not like Haruhi's arbitrary behavior was anything new. She'd probably been born with it. In five hundred years, they'll probably have a story going around about how she was proclaiming that the universe belonged to her the second she came out of the womb, just one of the many legends in the Haruhi Suzumiya chronicles. Well, who cares about that.

Haruhi and Tsuruya, walking at the front of the group, had hit it off at some point and were singing the chorus of Bryan Adams's "18 Til I Die" over and over in ridiculously loud voices. It was excruciatingly embarrassing to be an acquaintance walking behind them.

I'm amazed the silent black Nagato and reflector-board-carrying star Koizumi can tag along without bothering to keep their distance. You should learn from Asahina, walking along with her shoulders slumped and head down. And you should help share the load of stuff I'm carrying. We've been going uphill for quite a while now. I'm starting to understand how it feels to be a racing horse training by running uphill.

"Okay. We're here. This is my house," Tsuruya shouted as she stopped and stood in front of a house. Her voice was big, and her house was big too. Well, I assumed it was big. Since I couldn't actually see the house from the gate. But there was more than enough to support the notion. If you can't see the house from the gate, that must mean it's a great distance away, and if you look to the left and right, you find a wall looking like something from a samurai residence stretching as far as the eye can see. I wonder what kind of crimes you'd have to commit to live in a place like this.

"Here. Come on in."

Haruhi and Nagato must not have known what the word "restraint" meant, seeing as how they just barged on in as if it were their own home. Asahina appeared to have been here before, since there was no sign of surprise on her face when Tsuruya pushed her in.

"An old family that follows old customs. You can feel the refinement in the mysterious bearing of the place. You can feel its age," Koizumi said in a voice that didn't exactly sound filled with admiration. Are you some kind of extravagance reporter?

After crossing space large enough for a baseball triangle, we finally reached the entrance. Tsuruya took Asahina to the bathroom before leading us to her room.

This made my own bedroom look like something a cat would sleep in. A spacious, traditional Japanese-style room that was so big you wouldn't know where to sit. Except that I was apparently the only one troubled by any of this. Haruhi entered the room without a care, followed by Nagato and Koizumi.

"Nice room. This is good enough to film in. That's it. We'll say this is Koizumi's room. We'll shoot some scenes of him getting close with Mikuru here."

Haruhi was sitting on a cushion and looking through a rectangle formed by her fingers. Tsuruya's room was a simple tatami affair with a tea table as the only furniture.

I was attempting to copy Nagato, sitting next to me, by kneeling on the floor with my back straight, but after three minutes my legs couldn't take it anymore. Haruhi had been sitting cross-legged to begin with as she whispered something into Tsuruya's ear.

"Gaha! Hey, that sounds fun! Hold on a sec!"

And with that, Tsuruya, laughing cheerfully, zipped out of the room.

I put my thinking cap on. Is Tsuruya really a normal person? It's a widely held opinion that anyone able to get along with Haruhi is either abnormal or not human. It could just be that they happen to be on the same wavelength.

After a few minutes of waiting, Tsuruya returned. She brought Asahina as a gift. And it wasn't the usual Asahina, but an Asahina who had just gotten out of the bath. She was wearing a loose T-shirt that was probably borrowed from Tsuruya. Actually, the T-shirt was the only thing she was wearing.

"Ah . . . S-sorry to keep everyone waiting. . . ."

Asahina, with her hair still damp and skin flushed, hid behind Tsuruya as she entered the room before kneeling down straight and hunching up. The sleeves and shirt were too long for Asahina, which resulted in the T-shirt looking more like a one-piece dress — quite a wonderful effect. She'd forgotten to remove the contact, which meant her right eye was still silver, which would have been dangerous, but the fact that neither beams nor sharp wires would be shooting out meant I could breathe easy. It almost made me want to run to some shrine and worship Nagato, who still hadn't removed her hat.

"Here you go. Drink up."

The tray Tsuruya set on the floor was filled with enough glasses of orange-colored liquid for everyone in the room. In a flash Asahina drank half of the glass of orange juice handed to her by Tsuruya. She'd been the most active today, so she was probably pretty dehydrated.

As I also gratefully savored my juice, Haruhi had already downed hers in a single gulp and was crunching away at the remaining ice.

"Okay. We might as well film in this room while we're here."

After barely any rest, we were already starting to film the next scene.

Koizumi carried Asahina, pretending to be unconscious, into the room. For some reason, a futon was already spread on the floor. Koizumi laid Asahina down on the futon and stared at her sleeping face.

Asahina's face was fairly flushed, and her eyelashes were twitching. Koizumi placed a blanket over her defenseless body, crossed his arms, and sat down at her side.

"Unh . . . ," Asahina pretended to mumble in her sleep. Koizumi continued to watch her with a smile on his face.

Nagato, who apparently didn't have a part in this scene, was still drinking her orange juice behind Tsuruya and me. I zoomed in on Asahina's sleeping face as I gazed through the viewfinder. Haruhi didn't provide any instructions, so I was free to follow my own preferences. However, Haruhi continued issuing real-time instructions to the two leading stars.

"Mikuru, it's about time for you to wake up. Say your lines exactly the way I told you to."

". . . Unh —"

Asahina gradually opened her eyes and looked up at Koizumi in a daze.

"Are you awake?" asked Koizumi.

"Yes . . . Um, where am I . . ."

"My room."

Asahina sat up slowly. She looked like she had a fever, and her eyes couldn't seem to focus. She's behaving awfully sexy; is she acting?

"Th . . . thank you very much."

Haruhi immediately relayed the next instruction.

"Now, you two! Get your faces closer together! And then Mikuru closes her eyes and Koizumi puts his arm around her shoulder. Or just shove her down and kiss her!"

"Huh . . ."

For some reason, Asahina's mouth was half open in a stupor. Koizumi put his arm around Asahina's shoulder as instructed, which was when I could no longer hold myself back.

"Hold it. You're doing way too much abridging. And wait, why is there even a scene like this? What's going on here?"

"It's romantic moment. A love scene. You have to include stuff like this when you're doing a multiple time-slot program."

Moron. Is this supposed to be a two-hour drama that airs at 9 PM? And you, Koizumi. Why do you look like you're ready to act? If something like this gets screened, you'll find hundreds of curses in your shoe locker. Use your head.

The sound of cackling laughter made me turn around. Tsuruya was bent over with her nails digging into the tatami mat, laughing her head off.

"Haha — Mikuru's acting so funny!"

It's not funny. . . . At least, that's what I wanted to say, but it was clear that Asahina wasn't acting normally. She couldn't even hold up her head straight, her eyes were dazed, and her cheeks were flushed. And she wasn't even resisting Koizumi's arm around her shoulder. Not amusing at all.

"Uh . . . Koizumi, my head feels heavy . . . Ah."

As she said things that made me want to offer flowers to a certain mouse, Asahina was lurching around. I was wondering if she had been drugged when I realized something. My eyes went to her empty glass as Tsuruya laughed.

"Sorry. I mixed tequila into Mikuru's juice. I was told that some alcohol might help her acting get better."

Haruhi's sinister idea, huh? I was more angry than shocked. Don't secretly mix that kind of stuff in.

"Who cares. Mikuru looks really sexy right now. Makes for a better scene," said Haruhi.

You couldn't call this acting anymore. Asahina was staggering around. Her cheeks were flushed red below her closed eyes. I don't mind her looking sexy but I'm not too happy about her leaning up against Koizumi.

"Koizumi, just kiss her already. Of course, I mean on the lips!"

Hell no. You shouldn't be doing that to someone who can't even tell left from right in her current condition.

"Cut it out, Koizumi."

Koizumi appeared to ponder whether he should listen to the director or the cameraman. I'm gonna smack you. Either way, I lowered the camera. I don't intend to film such a scene and I don't intend to let such a scene be filmed.

Koizumi smiled as though to reassure me and moved away from the staggering leading lady.

"Director, this is too much for me to handle. And Asahina seems to have reached her limit."

". . . I'm perfectly fine, though . . . ," Asahina said while looking anything but perfectly fine.

"Honestly. I guess it can't be helped."

Haruhi puckered her lips like a duck's bill and approached the inebriated girl.

"Oh, you're still wearing the contact? That should have been off for this scene."

She whacked the back of Asahina's head.

"O . . . ouch," said Asahina as she held her head.

"That's no good, Mikuru! The contact's supposed to pop out when I whack your head. Let's try it again. Practice."

Whack.

"Ow."

Whack.

". . . Ugh," Asahina whimpered as she squeezed her eyes shut.

"Cut it out, stupid," I said as I grabbed Haruhi's arm. "How is this practice? What does this have to do with acting? How is any of this fun?"

"What is it? Don't stop me. I'm merely following convention."

"What convention? This isn't amusing at all. It's dumb. Asahina isn't your toy."

"I've decided that she is. Mikuru's my toy!"

The second I heard that, blood rushed to my head. It felt like I was seeing red. I seriously snapped. For a second, impulse overcame reason and my body was reacting unconsciously.

Somebody grabbed my wrist. Koizumi was shaking his head at me with narrowed eyes. I saw that Koizumi had stopped my right arm, which was when I noticed that my right hand was balled up in a fist. My right fist had been on the verge of punching Haruhi.

"What are you . . . !"

Haruhi glared at me with a glint in her eye as bright as the Pleiades.

"What do you have a problem with? You should just do as I say!

I'm the brigade chief and director and . . . Anyway, I won't allow you to go against me!"

I was seeing red again. Damn bitch. Let me go, Koizumi. Doesn't matter if you're dealing with animals or humans, anyone who refuses to listen deserves to be socked. Or else she'll spend the rest of her life as a prickly moron that everybody avoids.

"Pl-pl . . . please stop!" Asahina jumped in, speaking in a slurred voice. "You mustn't. Mustn't fight . . ."

Asahina, who had come between Haruhi and me, collapsed to the ground, face bright red. She put her arms around Haruhi's knees.

"Uh . . . *hic.* Everybody has to get along together . . . Or else . . . hmm — Oh, that's classified."

And with that, Asahina's eyes closed as she mumbled. And then her breathing grew regular as she fell asleep.

Koizumi and I were walking down the hill. We could see the pond we had been using below us.

The actress was no longer employable, so filming was called off. After leaving the sleeping Asahina in the hands of Tsuruya, Koizumi and I along with Nagato retired from the mansion, but for some reason Haruhi insisted on staying behind by herself, took the video camera from me, and turned her back on us. I didn't say a word as I gathered up our belongings. Tsuruya saw us off.

"Sorry, Kyon," Tsuruya said apologetically, but she soon smiled. "I got a little carried away there! Don't worry about Mikuru. I'll send her home later. Or she can even stay the night!"

Nagato trudged off the second she was through the gate. Doesn't seem like she has anything to say about all of this. That's how she is anyway. She never has anything to say about anything.

After five minutes of walking by my side silently, Koizumi opened his mouth.

"I expected you to be a more composed person."

That's what I thought too.

"We already have enough irregularities in the real world to deal with. I would rather you refrain from any actions that would lead to the creation of closed space."

Like I care. Isn't that what the fishy-sounding secret "Agency" or whatever is for? You people can deal with it.

"In regard to the prior incident, it would appear that Suzumiya was unconsciously restraining herself. Closed space has not appeared anywhere. This is a request from me. Please make amends with her tomorrow."

I decide what I'm going to do. I'm not going to do something because you told me to.

"Well, what's important now is to think about what to do about any effect she has had in real space."

Koizumi shamelessly changed the subject. I went along with it.

"Can't really do any thinking about it. I have no idea what's wrong with what."

"The theory is simple. Whenever Suzumiya has an idea, there is a ripple effect in the real world. Isn't that how it's been?"

I recalled the blue giants wreaking havoc in the gray world.

"Whenever Suzumiya says something, we have to respond accordingly. After all, that is our role in this world."

I remembered the glowing red balls. Koizumi spoke in a confident voice as he strolled along.

"We serve as Haruhi Suzumiya's tranquilizer. Her sedative."

"Well . . . guess that would apply to you."

"It also applies to you."

The mysterious former transfer student continued to smile.

"Closed space is our primary workplace. You are responsible for the real world. If you can keep Suzumiya calmed down, closed space will not appear. As a result of your efforts, my workload has decreased significantly in the past six months. I should thank you."

"Don't bother."

"Is that so? Then I won't."

We reached the road at the bottom of the hill. Koizumi broke the silence again.

"Incidentally, there's somewhere I'd like you to come with me right now."

"If I refuse?"

"We will reach the location shortly. You won't need to do anything there. Of course, this is not an invitation to closed space."

Koizumi abruptly raised his arm. A familiar black taxi came to a stop next to us.

"As I was saying."

Koizumi leaned against the backseat of the taxi. I stared at the back of the driver's head.

"At the present, there is a pattern to the situations involving you and Suzumiya. The basic framework involves you and the rest of us brigade members actualizing Suzumiya's whims."

"It's a pain."

"Indeed. However, we do not know how long the status quo will be maintained. A repetition of events is most likely one of Suzumiya's peeves.

"Though she appears to be having fun right now," continued Koizumi with a smile that lacked any sense of urgency.

"We must strive to keep Suzumiya's quirks within the contents of the movie."

"If you want to become a baseball player, you start by practicing swinging. If you want to become a shogi or go player, you start by memorizing rules. If you want to score the highest on final exams, you should start by having the resolve to stay awake all night with your eyes glued to your textbook. In other words, different methods can be applied to the concept of hard work. However, what kind of hard work is needed to eliminate Haruhi's mental delusions?

"If you tell her to stop, there'll be a mass outbreak of that stupid aggravating gray space. But if you just go along with her fantasies, there's a possibility they'll become reality.

"Either way leads to an extreme result. Does she not understand the concept of moderation? Well, I suppose that's what makes Haruhi Suzumiya Haruhi Suzumiya."

I noticed that you could see more green in the scenery outside the car. The taxi was driving a snaking uphill road. It led to the mountain the bus had taken us to yesterday.

Eventually, the car came to a stop in an empty parking lot. It was for visitors to the shrine. The shrine where Haruhi had turned a gun on the priest and doves yesterday. That's odd. There should be more people here on Sunday.

Koizumi exited the taxi first.

"Do you remember what Suzumiya said yesterday?"

"Like I'm going to remember every random thing she's said."

"You'll remember once we're there. Let's head inside." He then added, "It was already like this in the morning."

We ascended the stone stairs. We passed through here yesterday. The gate's at the top and there's a gravel path that leads to the shrine and that's where the flock of doves . . .

". . ." was my reaction.

There were doves bustling all around. A flock of birds pecking at the ground like a moving carpet. However, I couldn't be sure that these were the same doves as yesterday.

That would be because every single feather on the mass of doves was completely white.

". . . Did someone paint them?"

In just one night.

"There is no doubt that the white feathers on these doves are completely natural. They are the result of neither dyeing nor bleaching."

"Maybe they were really scared by Haruhi. Or someone brought a whole bunch of white doves and replaced the park birds."

"Infeasible. Who would so such a thing?"

Just throwing the idea out there. I've already come to my own conclusion. I just don't want to say it aloud.

This is what Haruhi said yesterday: *I'd prefer doves that are completely white, but I'm willing to take any color at this point.*

Obviously, she wasn't.

"That's how it is. This must be the result of an unconscious act by Suzumiya. We are fortunate that it happened a day later."

Possibly expecting us to feed them, the rustling doves came over to us. There weren't any other worshippers around.

"As you can see, Suzumiya's rampage is steadily progressing. The ill practices from the film production are advancing into the real world."

Wasn't Asahina shooting rays and wires from her eyes enough?

"Can't we just shoot Haruhi with a tranquilizer and let her sleep until the cultural festival's over?"

Koizumi responded to my proposal with a chuckle.

"It's plausible, but would you be willing to handle the aftermath when she wakes up?"

"No thanks."

It's not my duty to provide such service.

Koizumi shrugged. "What do we do then?"

"Isn't she God? You fanatics can deal with it."

Koizumi feigned a look of surprise.

"Suzumiya is God? My, who said such a thing?"

"You did?"

"Is that so?"

This guy's the one I should punch in the face.

Koizumi laughed and delivered his usual "Just kidding" before moving on.

"The fact of the matter is, I see no problem with labeling Suzumiya as 'God.' The general view within the Agency is to regard her as 'God.' Of course, there are dissidents. I would consider myself a skeptic as well. What I'm trying to say is that if she truly were God, she would not be living in this world, unaware of that fact. A Creator should be high above, performing occasional miracles and watching calmly as we scurry around."

I squatted down and picked up a feather that had fallen. I then began twirling the feather. The cries of the doves grew louder. Sorry, I didn't bring any bread crumbs.

"This is what I believe."

Koizumi was still talking to himself.

"Suzumiya was granted divine powers, and she is unaware of that fact. If a divine being really exists in this world, then Suzumiya would be a special human chosen by God. But she would still be human."

"I don't think it makes much difference whether she's human or not. Still, why does Haruhi unconsciously possess such baseless magical power? Enough to turn doves white? What's it for? Who's it for?"

"I haven't slightest idea. I do not know. Perhaps you do?"

Is he trying to pick a fight?

"Excuse me," Koizumi chuckled before continuing.

"Suzumiya builds, but at the same time, she destroys. Perhaps, our current reality was a failed effort. And perhaps Haruhi Suzumiya is the existence who has been given the mission of correcting this failed world."

Keep going.

"Which would mean that we are mistaken. Suzumiya is always in the right. We who interfere with her actions would be considered alien elements to this world. That's not all. In fact, every human besides Suzumiya would be mistaken."

Huh. Sounds bad, eh.

"The problem would be for those of us on the wrong side. When the world is reconstructed in its correct form, will we be a part of the new world? Will we be removed as bugs? Nobody knows the answer."

Don't say anything if you don't know the answer. Especially not in a tone that makes it sound like you know what you're talking about.

"But you could say, in a way, that she has been unable to effectively reconstruct the world. That would be because her conscious is suited to create. Suzumiya is a very positive person. However, what do you think would happen if that were reversed?"

It didn't look like he was going to shut up. I gave up and asked, "What will happen?"

"We don't know. However, it is easier to destroy than to create. I don't believe in that, so it should vanish. That's all it takes. Just like that, whatever she's referring to would cease to exist. She can cancel everything. It doesn't matter how strong a foe may appear, Suzumiya needs only to deny its existence and it will be destroyed. Be it magic or advanced technology. Regardless of what it may be."

"But Haruhi wouldn't reject it. Since that's what she's been waiting for."

"That is why we are concerned," Koizumi murmured in a voice that didn't sound very concerned. "I doubt we have any way of knowing whether Suzumiya is a god or a similar existence of some sort, but there is one thing we can be certain of. If she were to freely use her power, it would not matter if the world changed or not because no one would realize it. That's quite impressive. After all, Suzumiya herself would not realize it."

"Why?"

"Because Suzumiya is part of the world. Evidence that she is not the Creator. The God who created this world should be outside of it. However, she lives in the same world as the rest of us. And the fact that she can only cause incomplete changes is unnatural and extremely bizarre."

"From where I'm standing, you're the bizarre one."

Koizumi ignored me and continued.

"However, I am quite fond of the world we live in. A number of social contradictions exist, but humans should be able to deal with them over the course of time. The problem would be if there were a change such as Ptolemaic theory becoming accurate and the sun orbiting Earth. We must do what we can to prevent Suzumiya from believing such things. You returned from closed space because you were of a similar opinion, correct?"

I dunno. Beats me. I forgot already. I've locked away past memories I don't want to remember.

Koizumi smiled thinly. A self-mocking sort of smile.

"I spoke out of character. I must have sounded like a defender of justice convinced that we were protecting the world. Please excuse my outburst."

CHAPTER 5

It was Monday morning. Less than a week was left before the cultural festival, yet the atmosphere in our school was as relaxed as ever. Does this school really intend to hold a cultural festival? Shouldn't there be more activity? Everyone seems a little too laid-back. I was feeling pretty lousy as a result. And as I walked to the classroom, I came across something that made me feel even worse.

Koizumi was leaning against the wall in front of my classroom. You still have something to say after all that talking yesterday?

"Class 1-9 held play rehearsal early this morning. I just happened to be passing by."

I'd rather not have to see your smirking face this early in the morning.

"What is it? Don't tell me that stupid space ended up showing up again."

"No. It never appeared yesterday. It seems that Suzumiya is too busy feeling depressed to feel irritated."

"Why's that?"

"You should know the answer. . . . But allow me to explain. Suzumiya believed that you were the only one who would always be on her side, no matter what happened. You might complain and protest, but you would support her in the end. No matter what she did, you would still forgive her. Right?"

What do you mean, "right"? The only person capable of forgiving everything she does would be one of those ancient martyred saints. And just so you know, I'm neither a saint nor a great person. Just an ordinary, sensible individual.

"Did anything happen with Suzumiya?"

Like I'd let anything happen. Nothing's changed.

"Could you tell her to cheer up? White doves are relatively harmless. But if Suzumiya's mood continues to deteriorate, the doves at the shrine may be replaced by something that isn't very dove-like."

"Like what?"

"This wouldn't be so hard if we knew the answer to that. Would it not be fairly creepy if a swarm of slimy tentacle creatures were crawling around the shrine?"

"Just spread some salt around."

"That wouldn't solve the fundamental problem. Suzumiya is currently in a state of suspension. Thus far, she had been proactively altering reality through filming the movie. But after your incident yesterday, she's gone off on an opposite tangent. From positive to negative. There wouldn't be an issue if that were the end of it, but at this rate, things will get much worse."

"So. You want me to comfort her?"

"It's not that complicated. Simply kiss and make up."

"How does that even make sense? We're not even close or anything."

"Well. I expected you to have cooled down by now. Was I expecting too much?"

I kept my mouth shut.

I lost my cool yesterday because the goodness of my heart couldn't bear watching the tyrannical abuse of Asahina — or maybe not. Maybe it was just a result of calcium deficiency. Since after drinking a whole liter of milk last night, I woke up this morning to discover my rage had mysteriously evaporated. Though it could just be a placebo effect.

Still, why should I have to be the one to compromise? I'm pretty sure that everyone would agree that she was the one who went too far.

Koizumi was chuckling like a cat hacking up a hairball as he clapped my shoulder.

"I'm counting on you. Since as far as physical distance is concerned, you're the closest one to her."

As long as I never turned around, Haruhi, sitting right behind me, and I would never make eye contact. She appeared really interested in the weather today as she just sat there staring out the window until it was lunchtime.

On top of that, there must have been an epidemic or something because Taniguchi was in a bad mood as well.

"How was that a movie? Yesterday was such a waste of time."

Taniguchi cursed as he ate his box lunch. Haruhi was rarely ever in the classroom during breaks, and this was no exception. If she were here, this guy wouldn't be saying stuff like that. Timid people tend to speak loudly when the coast is clear.

"We're talking about Suzumiya here. This movie or whatever will just end up being trash. That's obvious."

I don't care what anyone else has to say. I don't consider myself to be a remarkable person and I don't see my name going down in history. I'm the kind of person who sits in a corner mumbling to himself. The kind who specializes in complaining about his mother's cooking when he can't even cook.

However, there was something I had to get off of my chest, so I did.

"You're the last person who should be saying that.

"Taniguchi, what have you been doing? At least Haruhi is trying to participate in the cultural festival. Even if she ends up causing trouble for a bunch of people, that still makes her better than someone who does nothing besides complain. Idiot. Apologize to all the Taniguchis in this country. It must be unpleasant for the other Taniguchis to have the same name as you."

"Now, now, Kyon."

Kunikida came between us. "He's just sulking. He really wanted to have more fun with Suzumiya and everyone else. He's jealous of you."

"Like hell I am," Taniguchi retorted as he glared at Kunikida. "I have no intention of joining that stupid group."

"Even though you tag along whenever you're invited? You were happy about it yesterday. You even canceled your plans for the day."

"Don't mention that, stupid."

So that's why Taniguchi's in a bad mood. He skipped his original plans to come yet he was sent packing after barely having any screen time. Plus he fell into the pond. I see. He deserves some sympathy. Although I'm not in the mood to offer any, seeing as how I'm pretty pissed myself.

I already knew that Haruhi's movie was so bad, it was unfit for viewing. She's just winging it full-speed as usual without any planning or thinking. Whatever she happens to want to film at that moment is what we film. No transition or direction. If all of this produced an amazing movie, that would be the work of a genius, and as far as I can see Haruhi doesn't have any talent as a director. Still, when other people start pointing that out to me — well, as for why it pisses me off . . .

"What's wrong, Kyon? Suzumiya seems to be in a worse mood than usual today. Did something happen?"

I did some thinking as I listened to Kunikida's voice.

I was no different from Taniguchi. I would do what Haruhi told me to do and then bitch about it. I could apply what I felt about him to myself. I had gotten fed up with griping about every little thing Haruhi did . . . but it's my duty. A job only I can do. Not because I don't want to let someone else do it, but because that's just how it is.

Food doesn't taste very good when you're eating while irritated. Now I feel bad about my mom making it for me. Damn that pukehead Taniguchi! It's all because you had to open your mouth. Now I feel like doing something I'll probably regret in the distant future.

What did I do?

I replaced the cover on my box lunch and dashed out of the classroom.

Haruhi was in the literary club room hooking the video camera up to the computer or something, but once she saw me suddenly open the door, she looked up in surprise. Was that curry bread in her left hand?

She hastily tossed her bread aside and reached behind her head to touch her hair — or so I thought, but then she untied her hair. Not sure why, but apparently she was in a rush to untie the clump of hair at the back of her head. I didn't get a good look, so I'll just think about it later. I said the words I needed to say right then.

"Hey, Haruhi."

"What is it?"

Haruhi had a look on her face like that of a cat ready for combat. I said straight to that face:

"Let's absolutely make this film a success."

It was a spur-of-the-moment thing. Even I may experience a high once or twice a year. That's probably why I snapped yesterday. It was just bad timing. And then today, the combination of Koizumi's strange conversation, Taniguchi's dumb face, and Haruhi looking depressed got me all agitated. If I hadn't done something about these pent-up urges, I might have started walking around smashing classroom windows, so I released it here instead. Why am I making excuses?

"Hmm," Haruhi said before continuing. "Of course. I'm the director after all. Success is guaranteed. I don't need you to tell me that."

So simple-minded. I was kind of expecting her to react in a somewhat laudable manner, but her eyes, shining brightly for reasons unknown, had been reignited with the flames of confidence. Way too simple. About as annoying as a mid-boss that keeps casting high-level healing spells on itself, but I didn't really care. The important thing is balance. A game where you just send a bunch of weak guys beyond in one blow and it's over . . . what was it again, that's it, doesn't have a catharsis. Not that I actually know what that means. Or it didn't mean anything to begin with. What I'm trying to say is that I don't want to see a cheerless Haruhi because it just weirds me out. Her mind is meant to always be engaged in a thousand-meter dash with no meaning, purpose, or destination. Since it seems that if she stops for some weird reason, she unconsciously causes even more random trouble. That's all.

. . . At least, that's what I believed at the time.

* * *

After school the same day.

"Couldn't you have worded that in a different way?" Koizumi asked.

"Sorry," I replied.

"When I asked you to cheer her up, I was expecting something with less . . . potential to create harm."

". . . Sorry."

"Instead of restoring the situation, you seem to have escalated it."

". . ."

"We won't be able to conceal everything at this rate."

Koizumi looked at me with gentle eyes as I reflected upon my actions. He didn't blame me, though I could sense a tone of distress in his voice. Guess that makes sense. The situation's definitely gotten worse, and it's apparently my fault.

Why is that? Hell if I know.

The cherry blossoms were in full bloom. We were walking down a cherry tree–lined path along the river. This was the riverwalk where Asahina had revealed her identity to me. Just to make sure, it's fall right now. Even if lingering traces of summer heat remain, Yoshino cherry trees bloom in spring. I don't have a problem if they start blooming early, but not six months early. There's no reason for cherry trees to tag along with the sun in going overboard.

Standing within the dancing cherry blossoms, Haruhi was the only one in full gear. Asahina, in her tight waitress outfit, was tottering around nervously. Probably because of all the out-of-season cherry blossom–watchers around.

"How convenient! I was just thinking about how I'd like a shot with cherry blossoms. This abnormal weather has perfect timing!" Haruhi exclaimed, sending spit flying, as she forced Asahina to strike random poses.

Guess it's no good. When humans act on a moment's impulse, it'll always come back to haunt them. It feels like I've been repeatedly learning this lesson over the past six months. A very negative lesson where I went "Shouldn't have done that," instead of "If only I had done that." Someone lend me a gun. And I don't mean a model gun.

It appears that the buds on the cherry trees began sprouting around noon, and by evening they were in full bloom. The local news station even sent down a crew to report on this unusual autumn occurrence. I wish they'd just assume that this happens every once in a while. The strange global climate in the past few years would be the underlying cause. Just leave it at that, okay?

"That what Suzumiya appears to believe," Koizumi, who had been walking next to Asahina down by the riverbank just a moment ago, remarked. The shot of Koizumi, who merely looked good, and Asahina, who was purely good, next to each other was incredibly well suited for pissing off every single male on the planet. It left me with an unpleasant feeling.

Nagato had nothing to say about the cherry blossoms and no expression on her face either. She simply stared at the blossoms with their whacked-out internal clock. The sight of pink petals on her black mantle created a slight contrast effect. Wonder if she knows about the white doves.

"That's it! Let's catch a cat!" Haruhi said out of the blue. "Witches have familiars. And cats are the best fit! Is there a black cat around anywhere? One with glossy fur."

"Hold on. Wasn't Nagato's initial setting an evil alien?"

"Just find a cat! That's the image I have in my mind right now. Where's a good place to find a cat?"

"Probably a pet store."

Oddly enough, Haruhi responded to my slapdash remark with a compromise.

"A stray cat works. It'd be a pain to try to borrow one that's for sale or has an owner. Shouldn't we be able to find a whole bunch lying around on some vacant piece of land? Yuki, do you know?"

"I know."

Nagato nodded her head ever so slightly before she started walking off like a religious leader guiding us to the Promised Land. I guess there isn't anything Nagato doesn't know. If I ask her where the coin purse I dropped five years ago went, she might give me an answer. My entire life savings at the time, five hundred yen, was inside, I believe.

After fifteen minutes of walking, we arrived behind the fancy apartment building where Nagato lived by herself. There was a well-maintained lawn shaded by trees that blocked the view from outside. A number of cats were gathered there. They appeared to be strays, but none of them appeared to be afraid of people, seeing as how none of them ran away when we approached. They even started following us around. Maybe they were expecting to be fed. Haruhi picked one of the cats up.

"There aren't any black cats here. We'll just go with this one then."

It was a calico, and a male one to boot. But Haruhi apparently had no idea how rare that was and showed no surprise at the result from her random sampling.

"Okay, Yuki. This is your partner. Get along now."

Nagato silently accepted the calico cat Haruhi was holding up. She showed as much emotion as if she were accepting a tissue. The cat didn't show any emotion either.

We promptly began filming on the spot again. We were still behind the apartment building. I didn't think she really cared about location anymore. My video camera was filled with a bunch of erratic, spur-of-the-moment cuts. It better not be my job to edit this all into a single story.

"Yuki, attack Mikuru!"

Nagato nodded in response to Haruhi's orders, in an awkward stance. A black-garbed mage with a cat riding on her left shoulder. The cat obviously looked too heavy to ride there. It helped that the calico was obediently clinging to Nagato, but Nagato had to tilt not just her neck, but her whole body, to keep her balance and prevent the cat from falling off. And while maintaining that unnatural posture, she waved her wand at Asahina.

"Take this."

I'm guessing that magical rays will be shooting out of Nagato's wand for this scene.

". . . Ahh —"

Asahina's agonized acting.

"Okay, cut!" Haruhi yelled in a satisfied tone as I stopped recording. Koizumi lowered the reflector board.

"We'll make it so that the cat talks. He's supposed to be a mage's familiar. He can deliver a sarcastic insult or something."

Unbelievable.

"Your name is Shamisen. Come on, Shamisen, say something!"

Like he's going to start talking. Or yeah, please don't start talking.

Perhaps my prayer was heard, because the calico cat with the ominous name Shamisen did not suddenly start speak Japanese. Instead, it started grooming its tail, completely ignoring Haruhi's order. The natural reaction, but it still left me feeling relieved.

"Looking good."

Haruhi smiled with satisfaction as she checked the film we'd shot today. Hard to believe she was looking depressed just this morning. Being able to move on quickly is a good thing. That, alone, I can admire her for.

"Kyon, you're responsible for taking care of that cat."

She delivered the absurd command to me as she folded up her director's chair.

"Give him a warm reception when you get home. We'll need him for future filming, so do a proper job of taming him. Teach him a trick or two by tomorrow. Yeah, like jumping through a ring of fire or something."

I'd have to say that being able to sit still on Nagato's shoulder puts him in the high-performing category of cats.

"That's all for today. We'll be headed into the final stage tomorrow! The filming is smoothly approaching the climax and everybody's in perfect shape! Make sure you get plenty of rest for tomorrow."

After Haruhi dismissed us with a wave of the megaphone, she left by herself, humming the ending theme from *Blade Runner.*

"Whew —"

Asahina and I sighed in unison. As for the other two, Koizumi had the reflector board under his arm as he prepared to go home, and Nagato was looking at Shamisen the way you look at a ballpoint pen with no ink.

I crouched down and petted the calico on his head.

"Good work. I'll treat you to a can of cat food later. Or would you prefer dried sardines?"

"Either's fine with me."

Spoken in a clear baritone voice. It didn't belong to anyone there. I looked at the gaping faces of Koizumi and Asahina before turning to Nagato's blank face. All three were staring at the same spot. My feet.

A calico cat sat there looking up at me with round, black eyes.

"Hey, now," I said. "Was that Nagato just now? I wasn't talking to you. I was asking the cat."

"That was my belief. Which is why I responded. Did I say something wrong?"

The cat spoke.

"What a quandary."

That was Koizumi talking.

"I'm shocked. A talking cat . . ."

That was Asahina.

". . ."

Nagato remained silent as she stood holding Shamisen. As for Shamisen himself . . .

"I cannot fathom why you people are so surprised."

He was talking as he clung to Nagato's shoulder.

"Must be something along the lines of a cat-demon-type creature. Don't they say that this is what happens after they've lived so many years?"

"I do not know the answer. I place no value in having a sense of time. I have no interest in differentiating between the present and past."

A cat talking is already weird enough, but he's sounding like an academic. Pretty cheeky for something with paws. Where's the nearest shamisen shop? Is it in the Yellow Pages?

"Indeed, from your perspective, it may appear that I am emitting sounds that resemble human speech. However, parrots and parakeets are capable of doing the same. How can you be sure that the sounds I emit are meant to express the meaning of the words you hear?"

What's he talking about?

"It's, yeah, because you're answering my questions."

"Is it not possible that the sounds I am emitting simply conform by coincidence to the conditions of a response to your question?"

"If you accept that, wouldn't that mean fellow human beings could be talking without actually holding a conversation?"

Why am I having a serious discussion with a cat?

The stray calico Shamisen licked his front paw and scratched under his ear. "You are absolutely correct. You and the young lady over there could engage in actions that would make it appear as though you were holding a conversation, but nobody would have any way of knowing whether or not accurate communication occurred," Shamisen said in an oddly rough voice.

"Since people may or may not say what they really mean in different situations," said Koizumi.

You keep your mouth shut.

"When you put it that way, it does . . . make sense," said Asahina.

Sorry, but could you also keep your mouth shut?

After examining the cats on the lawn one by one, we learned that every one besides Shamisen could only meow. Apparently, this calico cat was the only one to benefit from a sudden ability to speak a human language. Why was that?

It's that idiot's fault.

"The current situation does not look very encouraging," Koizumi offered as he elegantly carried his mug to his lips. "We appear to have underestimated Suzumiya."

"What do you mean?" asked Asahina in a hushed voice.

"I fear that the setting within Suzumiya's movie is becoming the conventional reality of this world. Events transpiring within her movie are becoming reality. At this rate, they will become a normal sight in our world. Like Asahina shooting lasers or cats talking. If she wishes to shoot a scene with a giant meteorite falling, it may really happen."

The four SOS Brigade members sans Haruhi were gathered in the café in front of the station. Koizumi proposed the establishment of an emergency joint headquarters for the purpose of dealing with Haruhi, and the rest of us agreed. It would appear that the situation was seriously deteriorating at a rapid pace. On the outside, we would have looked like a group of high-schoolers merrily engaged in idle chat (except that Koizumi was the only one smiling), but our meeting was about as suspicious as the evil ringleaders in a tokusatsu getting together to discuss how to seal away the good guys' special attacks. I should mention that Shamisen was waiting outside by some shrubbery after being instructed not to talk or respond to anybody. The cat simply said "Very well" without any sign of displeasure as he obediently hid under the shade of an evergreen tree by the road and watched us go.

"What will happen . . ."

Asahina looked remarkably solemn. The poor thing looked especially worn out. She was the one who'd suffered the most as a result of Haruhi's movie. There was no change in Nagato's default blank expression. And she was still dressed in black.

Koizumi spoke as he sipped his café au lait.

"If there's one thing we've learned, it would be that it is a bad idea to leave Suzumiya alone to do as she pleases."

"We don't need you to tell us that."

I downed my glass of water in one go. I'd already finished the apple tea I'd ordered.

"Isn't that why we're trying to solve the problem of how to stop Haruhi?"

"That's easy to say, but who could possibly cancel the production of this movie at this point? At the very least, I do not believe I would have a chance."

Neither do I.

Once Haruhi's engine is running, she's going to keep on going until it's turned off. Maybe she's related to those fish that die if they stop swimming. Maybe we could trace her family tree and find tuna or bonito among her ancestors.

Nagato silently drank her cinnamon tea looking like she wasn't thinking about anything at all. Maybe she really isn't thinking about anything at all. Or maybe it's because she already knows everything so she doesn't need to think. Or she's just a poor talker. After six months, I still have no idea what she's ever thinking about.

"Nagato, what do you think? Any opinion?"

". . ."

Nagato soundlessly returned her cup to the saucer and smoothly turned to look at me.

"Unlike the previous incident, Haruhi Suzumiya has not disappeared from this world."

Her voice sounded like it was freeze-dried.

"The Data Overmind has determined that is sufficient."

Koizumi gracefully placed a hand on his forehead.

"But this is a problem for us."

"There is no problem for us. Rather, we welcome the outbreak of change in our subject of observation."

"Really?"

Koizumi quickly gave up on Nagato and turned back to me.

"Then we need to decide what genre Suzumiya's movie will fall under."

Well, it looks like he's going to stop making sense again.

"The makeup of a story can be roughly assigned to one of three classifications. One that takes place within the framework of the story, one that destroys the framework and creates a new framework, or one that destroys the framework and restores it again."

And he's making a speech or something. Huh? What's this guy talking about? That would be the general reaction from the audience. Asahina, you shouldn't be listening to him so earnestly.

"Incidentally, we exist within the framework, so we can only learn about this world through logically thought-out conjecture or observational perception."

You keep mentioning framework. What do you even mean by that?

"For example, let us consider the 'reality' we exist in. I am speaking of the world we live in. On the other hand, the movie Suzumiya is producing would be considered fiction."

No kidding.

"The perceived problem is that events within fiction are having an effect on 'reality.'"

Miracle Mikuru Eye, doves, cherry blossoms, cat . . .

"We must guard against the infringement of fiction into reality."

Koizumi always looked so cheerful when he talked about stuff like this. His sunny face was practically beaming. I resisted by having a gloomy expression on my face.

"Suzumiya's strange powers are being actualized by using the production of this film as a filter. To guard against that, we must make Suzumiya understand that fiction is just fiction. Since at the moment, she has managed to unconsciously blur the distinction."

She must really be on a roll.

"We need to use a logical process to prove that fictional events are not real. We must shape this movie into a rational, calm affair."

"How are we supposed to justify a cat talking?"

"We won't be justifying anything. That would merely lead to the construction of a world where cats talk. In our 'reality,' cats do not talk. We must emphasize that there is something wrong with a talking cat. Because a world where cats can talk cannot possibly be a part of our world."

"But it's okay for aliens, time travelers, and espers?"

"Yes, of course. Because they already do exist. That is considered normal in our world. There just happens to be a condition that Suzumiya must not know about it."

Really?

"Let us pretend that there is an entity watching our world from afar. As far as this effeminate creature is concerned, the 'real' world would be, as you mentioned, one free of any paranormal or supernatural phenomena — a world where aliens, time travelers, and espers do not exist — which means that our current 'reality' would be viewed as a fictional world."

So that's the identity of your God, huh?

"However, that would be the perspective from the outside. You are already aware of the supernatural beings — such as myself and Nagato — that exist in this world. And in order to live in this world, you must accept reality from within the framework. Your concept of reality has changed in the past year."

"I might have been better off not knowing."

"Are you sure about that? Well, one thing is certain. Suzumiya's current condition is similar to your prior one. In other words, her perception of reality has not yet changed. While she may say differently, deep down she does not believe in the existence of supernatural beings. She personally witnessed closed space and Celestials yet she believes that incident to be a dream. Dreams are fictional. Which is why this 'reality' still remains our reality."

Which means what?

"Yes, which is why if fiction continues becoming reality, Suzumiya will recognize it as 'reality' and talking cats will become accepted as a part of 'reality.' It's considered weird for a cat to talk, so the realization of talking cats would require the reconstruction of this world. Suzumiya would create a world where talking cats would not be considered strange. It would most likely not be a world out of science fiction. Based on her pattern of thinking, she would probably find that too much trouble. The world would simply fall under the laws of fantasy. Talking cats exist. That's all that needs to be said. No need for any excuses as to why cats can talk. Because cats will have become talking animals to begin with."

Koizumi set down his mug and rubbed the ceramic edge with his finger.

"That would be a problem. The principles our world was built on would be turned upside down. I happen to respect what the human race has accomplished through observation and experimentation. On top of that, nobody has ever observed a cat spontaneously talking without any outside influence, which means that nobody would expect it to happen. It would be regarded as a bizarre anomaly in this world."

"What about you guys? Couldn't you say the same thing about espers?"

"Yes, that is why we would be considered deviations that disturb the established laws of the world. We exist because of Suzumiya. Which means that the same can be said for this talking cat. An existence derived by Suzumiya for the purpose of appearing in the movie. It would appear that a link is attempting to form between the contents of Suzumiya's movie and the real world. At least, that's what we've learned."

"So now we know. Anything we can do about it?"

"First of all, we must decide on a genre for the movie."

I seriously want to tell him to cut the crap already. Sure, you may enjoy delivering pretentious long speeches, but try to consider how your audience might feel. This is about as bad as an address from the principal at a morning assembly. See, Asahina's been looking kind of gloomy for a while now.

However, Koizumi apparently hadn't done enough talking.

"If this were a fantasy world, cats talking, Asahina shooting beams from her eyes, and other such phenomena would require no explanation. Because in such a world, that would be how it always has been."

I looked outside the window and made sure Shamisen was still there.

"However, if there were a reason for talking cats and Mikuru Beams to exist, that in itself would make this a different world. Cats were talking and Asahina was shooting beams in reality, but we weren't aware of it. Their existence would be proven through observation. But in that instance, our world would be altered. From a world without supernatural phenomena to a world that includes supernatural phenomena. The real world as we knew it would become a falsity."

I sighed. It didn't look like he was ever going to stop talking.

"So basically, if cats can talk, there is a reason why cats can talk. Is that what you're trying to say? But in that case, what about you, Nagato, and Asahina? Wouldn't you and the girls be classified as supernatural phenomena?"

"From your perspective perhaps. It is a self-evident truth. From your perspective, the world has already changed. Your perception of the world has changed since you entered high school, has it not? You are already aware of the existence of beings like us, are you not?"

"What are you trying to tell me?"

"Let us return to topic of the film. At this point, what Suzumiya is attempting to make would probably be classified as fantasy. Within the movie, the cat talks and Asahina and Nagato use magical powers without any explanation. That's just how it works. That's enough."

"So we just have to give the cat-demon, time-traveling waitress, and evil mage a reason to exist?"

"But it isn't so simple. In fact, things would worsen if we did give them a reason to exist. If an observer were to recognize the change within the world of the story between the start and end, it would be the same as accepting their existence. The world would change so that talking cats would be allowed to exist. I can't say that I would welcome the addition of further complications to this world."

Neither would I. Only Nagato's people wouldn't mind.

"I mentioned earlier that we needed to decide on a genre. I would like to offer the name of a genre at this point. This genre has the potential to disassemble all of the puzzles and supernatural phenomena with rational explanation and return this distorted world to its original state. The only genre where the world is restored at the end to its starting condition and all enigmatic phenomena are eliminated through rational means."

"What's that?"

"Mystery. Especially classic mystery. If you utilize the methods of this genre, phenomena that were hard to believe will become just that, phenomena that were hard to believe, without any need for bringing out supernatural elements. Talking cats and Asahina's killer beams could be explained as being the result of some sort of trick. Our reality would remain unchanged."

The café waitress came to take our cups, purposely ignoring Asahina the whole time. Once she left, Koizumi continued.

"A cat that can speak a human language obviously goes against the common sense of this world. Nevertheless, a talking cat exists here. Something that should not exist does exist. That is excruciatingly inconvenient for our world."

He flicked a drop of condensation on his glass.

"To resolve this situation, we must devise a rational ending for the movie. A conclusion that addresses the presence of talking cats, time travelers, and alien mages and can be accepted by everybody — more importantly, Suzumiya — in a logical manner."

"Does such a thing exist?"

"It does. A conclusion that can transform every illogical occurrence into a something ordinary in a relatively simple manner."

"Name it."

"It was all just a dream."

". . ."

Silence fell. Upon all of us. Eventually, Koizumi spoke.

"That wasn't intended as a joke . . ."

I directed a scornful look at the gentleman twisting a forelock of hair around his fingers.

"You think Haruhi will accept that? Lies and truths aside, she's pretty serious about winning that award. And you want to say it was all just a dream? I'm pretty sure she's not dumb enough to want to make such a retarded movie."

"How she feels is not relevant. This resolution was determined by our needs. Deeming that everything that happened within the movie was a dream, lie, or mistake is the best way to settle the matter."

For you maybe. It might be better for me too. But what about

Haruhi? She may have already thought up a spectacular, at least in her mind, last scene to use for an ending.

Besides, I don't want to touch the subject of dreams again. The same goes for your boring, arbitrary expositions.

I stopped by a general store on the way home. I bought the cheapest litter box and a can of cat food that was on sale. I also asked for a receipt, just in case. Shamisen was washing his face with his paws as he waited. I walked off. The cat followed.

"Okay. Don't say a single word at home. Behave like a cat."

"I do not understand what you mean when you say to behave like a cat, but I shall do as you request."

"Don't talk. Always respond with meow."

"Meow."

Upon seeing me arrive home with a stray cat, my sister's and mother's eyes grew wide. I gave a made-up explanation that "his owner's an acquaintance who went on a trip so I have to take care of him for a week" and received their ready consent. My sister was especially happy and began petting Shamisen all over. The cat-demon responded by obediently repeating the sound "meow." Guess that's not very cat-like either.

The night safely passed. I had to go to school again in the morning. I was worried about leaving Shamisen alone so I brought him along. As I urged him to get into the duffel bag, Shamisen responded, "Very well then, I suppose," in an arrogant tone before entering. I let him out by the school gate.

Only a few days remained before the cultural festival, and the atmosphere of chaos at our school had been steadily growing, as though it were linked with Haruhi's fervor. It made me wonder what the lack of energy up till yesterday had been about.

It was early in the morning, and I could already hear noise-makers and singing. There were also people around making signs and billboards. There was even a group of people wandering around in weird costumes that made you wonder what they were even planning on doing. As things stood, a slider or two could join in without feeling out of place. The only people without any motivation were the members of 1-5 probably. Maybe Haruhi sucked all the motivation out of the class.

I entered the classroom to find that Haruhi was already in her seat, scribbling furiously in a notebook.

"Did you finally feel like writing a script?" I asked as I reached my seat. Haruhi snorted as she raised her chin.

"No. This is a tagline for the movie."

"Show me."

I picked up the notebook and glanced over the page.

"Loaded with precious, punctiliously confidential, absolutely secret images of Mikuru Asahina! You'll absolutely regret missing this! The most talked-about film of the year presented by the SOS Brigade! Crowds will come flocking!"

I'll refrain from mentioning how uselessly sensational it is or how there are only two months left in the year, but all this really says is that Asahina will be involved. If someone can read this tagline and imagine what the movie will be like, I'll respect that person for all the wrong reasons. Well, I'm the one filming everything and I don't even know what the movie is about yet so I can't really complain. Maybe Haruhi doesn't know either? Whatever the case, I'm impressed she was able to spell "punctiliously" without looking at a dictionary.

"I'll print off a bunch of flyers and pass them out on the day of the festival. Yep, they'll work out great! Okabe won't complain about being dressed up as a bunny if it's the cultural festival, right?"

No, I think he'll complain. This is a strict prefectural high school. Stop doing things that give our teacher stomach pains.

"Besides, Asahina will be busy with her class's refreshment stand. Koizumi and Nagato probably have stuff to do with their own classes. The only people who don't have anything to do that day are you and me."

Haruhi looked at me with suspicious eyes.

"So you want to dress up in a bunny outfit?"

How did you come to that conclusion? You can handle it by yourself. I'll stand behind you holding up a billboard.

"By the way, did you know? There aren't that many days left till the cultural festival. The festival's this Saturday and Sunday."

"I know that."

"Really? You seemed pretty relaxed so I thought you might have gotten the date wrong."

"I'm not relaxed at all. At this very moment, I'm trying to come up with catch lines."

"There's something that needs to be done before you start thinking about advertising. When will the movie be finished?"

"Soon. We just need to shoot a few missing scenes, edit everything together, dub in voices and music, add visual effects, and it'll be done."

That's a surprise. From my perspective as the cameraman, I'd have to say that there would be more scenes missing than not. Exactly what kind of movie does the director intend this to be? Plus the work that has to be done after the filming sounds like it'll take far more time than we've spent so far. Though it could just be my misconception.

* * *

It was during the break between third and fourth period.

"Kyon!"

A ridiculously loud voice rang across the classroom, making everyone still there jump. I reflexively looked to see Tsuruya peeking through the door. I could barely see Asahina's soft hair next to her.

"Come over here for a sec."

I dashed over as if drawn in by Tsuruya's smile. Haruhi was still following her practice of disappearing the second break began so she wasn't in the classroom. She was probably wandering around school somewhere. How convenient.

As I went out into the hallway, Tsuruya tugged on my sleeve.

"Mikuru has something to tell you!" she shouted in a voice you probably could have heard on the opposite side of the building as she gave Asahina a smack in the back. "Come on, Mikuru. Give that to Kyon!"

With trembling hands, Asahina handed me a fluttery sheet of paper.

"This is . . . um, a d-d-discount voucher."

"It's for our class's yakisoba café," added Tsuruya to explain further.

I gratefully accepted it. It was basically like a coupon. According to the signed words printed on the paper, you would get a thirty-percent discount if you brought this paper.

"Please invite your friends to come along!"

Asahina bowed her head as Tsuruya laughed with a mouth as wide as a comic-book character's.

"That's all! See ya!"

As Tsuruya merrily walked off, Asahina moved to follow but immediately ran back to where I was. Tsuruya chuckled at the sight and stopped and stood in a waiting stance.

Asahina joined her fingers as she peeked up at me.

". . . Kyon."

"What is it?"

"You really shouldn't trust what Koizumi says. . . . I realize that this makes Koizumi sound like a bad person . . . which isn't my goal . . . but still . . ."

"You mean the stuff he says about Haruhi being God?"

I don't believe any of that.

"I, well . . . have a different idea about that. Basically, that is . . . it's different from Koizumi's interpretation."

Asahina breathed deeply before looking at me with upturned eyes.

"There's no doubt that Suzumiya has the power to alter the present. However, I don't believe she's changing the structure of the world. The world was like this to begin with. It wasn't created by Suzumiya."

Well, well . . . A view that totally rejects Koizumi's.

"I believe that Nagato also has a different view."

Asahina entwined her fingers before her uniform.

"Um . . . It might be rude to say this . . ."

Tsuruya was grinning as she watched us from a distance. The look on her face was like that of a mother swallow urging her chick to leave the nest. I think she misunderstood what was going on.

Asahina spoke her words in an unsophisticated tone.

"What Koizumi is saying is different from what we believe. It would be improper to tell you to well . . . not trust him . . . but, um . . ."

She waved her hands frantically.

"I'm sorry. I'm bad at explaining things, and there are restrictions on what I can say. . . . Um . . ."

She went through a cycle of hanging her head and looking back up at me.

"Koizumi has his own circumstances and theories. The same goes for us. And probably for Nagato as well."

Asahina gazed at me with a face so determined, she must have mustered all the willpower in her body. She's still cute when she looks serious. As I shook from the emotion of being able to see her face up close, I answered confidently.

"I know. How could Haruhi possibly be God, right?"

If the money I throw in whenever I visit a temple goes to her, I might as well set up Asahina as the founder of a new religion. It'll probably attract more believers too. I'd give it a double seal of approval.

"I find your view a lot easier to understand than Koizumi's."

Asahina had a little smile on her face. If sweet peas could smile, it'd probably look something like this.

"Mmm. Thank you. But I don't hold anything against Koizumi. Please understand that."

After delivering that odd statement with upturned eyes, she dashed off as though she were running away. With a wave of her small hand, she chased after Tsuruya like a spot-billed duckling following its mother.

It would probably be a good idea to get some work done. And with that thought, I headed to the club room to fiddle with the computer, wondering why such an admirable thought had popped into my mind, to find somebody already inside, wearing a pointy hat and black mantle while reading a book.

Before I could say a word . . .

"Mikuru Asahina's tenet is believed to be as follows," Nagato began, as though she had read my mind.

"Haruhi Suzumiya is not the Creator. She did not create this world. The world always existed in its current form. Supernatural entities such as ESP, temporal deviations, and conceptual alien organisms were not born as a result of Haruhi Suzumiya's wishes. They always existed. Haruhi Suzumiya's role is to discover such entities without being aware of their identity, and she has wielded that power for the past three years. However, her discoveries do not lead to self-recognition. She is able to detect abnormalities in the world, but she is by no means able to recognize them. That is because elements exist to prevent such recognition."

Her lips, never smiling, spoke the words plainly. Nagato stared into my eyes and said the following before shutting her mouth.

"That would be us."

"So Asahina, for a reason different from Koizumi's, would also be inconvenienced by Haruhi finding mysterious phenomena?" I asked.

"Yes."

Nagato returned her eyes to the open book. She didn't seem very interested in our conversation.

"She has come to this space-time to protect the future space-time she belongs to."

I have a feeling she just said something really important in passing.

"Haruhi Suzumiya is considered a variable to Mikuru Asahina's space-time, and in order to maintain the stability of the future, it is necessary to input the correct values. Mikuru Asahina's role is to regulate those values."

Nagato flipped the page without making a sound. She continued without even a blink of those hard, black eyes.

"Itsuki Koizumi and Mikuru Asahina have differing roles in mind for Haruhi Suzumiya. They can never accept the opposite side's interpretation. As far as they are concerned, a divergent theory would shake the very foundations of their existence."

"Wait. Koizumi said that his ESP showed up three years ago."

Nagato immediately responded to my query.

"There is no guarantee that Itsuki Koizumi is telling the truth."

I recalled that handsome smiling face in my mind. No guarantee indeed. Koizumi's theory just happens to conveniently explain everything that's happened to me. Who can say if he's right? The fact of the matter is, Asahina told me not to believe him. But the same goes for Asahina's theory. Nobody can guarantee that Asahina's answer is correct.

I looked at Nagato. Everything Koizumi has said may have been a downright lie. Asahina may not have realized that her view was a lie. But this composed alien didn't look like she'd be able to lie.

"What do you think about all of this? Which one's correct? What was that potential-for-autoevolution thing you were talking about anyway?"

The black-garbed bookworm was completely devoid of emotion.

"Any truth I may tell you will be unable to grant you solid proof."

"What's that?"

However, that was when I saw a truly rare sight. Nagato had a hesitant expression on her face. As I stood astonished, she responded.

"There is no guarantee that I am telling the truth."

And with that, she set down her book and left the club room, leaving the following words.

"Not for you, at least."

The bell began to ring.

I don't get it.

Normally, you wouldn't, right?

Koizumi and Nagato don't talk in a way that can be easily

understood by other people. It makes me wonder if they're doing it on purpose. They should at least put a little effort into trying to summarize what they're saying to something simpler. Or they'll be speaking to deaf ears. Nobody will bother to listen.

I walked along with my arms crossed as a group of people dressed in stateless medieval outfits ran past me and turned the corner. Nagato, in her black outfit, could probably join in without looking out of place. Maybe some class or club doesn't want to yield to Haruhi and is filming their own fantasy movie. Lucky them. They're probably having a fun time filming their movie without having to deal with any of the problems plaguing me. And they probably have a director who actually has common sense when it comes to issuing commands.

I sighed and returned to the 1-5 classroom.

Haruhi was the only one who believed filming was going well, as the expressions of gloom on the faces of Asahina, Koizumi, and myself gradually escalated.

A number of things appeared to be happening as the filming progressed. The next thing we knew, the model gun fired water bullets instead of BBs, Asahina shot dangerous crap from her eyes every time Haruhi brought a different-colored contact (the gold one shot out rifle darts and the green one shot out micro black holes), which would lead to her being bitten by Nagato, the cherry blossoms that had bloomed fell to the ground the next day, the white doves at the shrine turned into passenger pigeons, which were supposed to be extinct, a few days later (Koizumi told me this in secret), and the Earth's precession was a little off (according to Nagato).

Everyday life was falling apart around us.

I dragged my exhausted body home to be met by the whiskered animal opening his mouth.

"So I simply need to keep my mouth shut around that hyper girl."

The calico was sprawled on my bed in a posture resembling the Sphinx.

"So you do understand." I gently grabbed Shamisen's long tail. The cat slid the tail out of my grasp with a swish.

"You all were behaving in a manner that suggested as much. I also had a premonition that allowing her to hear me speak would be inconvenient."

"That's what Koizumi says."

A cat talked. Meaning that you would need a reason to explain why it wouldn't be strange for a cat to talk. The simple way to put it is that you would apparently need to reconstruct the world in a way so that talking cats wouldn't be considered strange. What would that world be like? What would the cast be like?

Shamisen yawned and began grooming his tail.

"There are many kinds of cats. Isn't it the same with humans?"

"It'd be nice if you went into detail about what your 'many kinds' exactly entailed."

"What would be the point in knowing that? I doubt you could ever fully become a cat, much less understand the mentality of one."

I'm fed up with every last one of them.

I was planning on taking a bath when my sister came to my room to inform me that I had a visitor.

I wondered who it might be as I went down the stairs. The one who had finally come all the way to my home was Koizumi. I went outside into the night to deal with him. It'd be a bad idea to let him into my room with his endless talking. And I sure as hell didn't want to be faced with the prospect of being doubled up on by him and Shamisen in some incomprehensible discussion of the abstract.

As expected, Koizumi began babbling by himself about some kind of theory. He even said the following.

"Suzumiya has no interest in detailed background explanations or subplot. She simply goes with whatever feels more fun, and that's enough reason for her. There is no rational resolution, careful composition, or fancy foreshadowing. You could say that she has created a rather transient story. She hasn't given any thought to a resolution. It is possible that the movie may end unfinished."

And that would be a problem, huh? Based on what you've said, if the movie ends halfheartedly, this messed-up reality will become our new reality. We have to force Haruhi to accept a conclusion in her mind, and that conclusion must conform to reality. And we're the ones who have to come up with such a conclusion. Haruhi doesn't think, and even if she were to, the result would always be chaos. If that's the case, we might as well do the thinking for her. Still, why do I have to rack my brain for such a reason? Anybody out there who can shoulder this curse for me?

"If such a person were to exist . . ."

Koizumi shrugged.

"That person would have appeared before us long ago. Therefore, we must do something about the situation. I'm especially looking forward to your efforts."

Efforts toward what? Start by explaining that to me.

"We have a problem with the world becoming fiction from a logical standpoint. Asahina may also have a problem with it. Her people follow their own logic. I'm not really sure about Nagato, but observers merely need to take in results. They will simply accept whichever theory wins out in the end. They have no problem with the Earth being blown to pieces, as long as Suzumiya remains."

The outdoor lamp illuminated Koizumi's business-like expression.

"The truth is that our Agency and Asahina's factions are not the only ones with theories centered on Suzumiya. There are many others. I would love to give you a digest of the disputes and bloody battles to the death going on under the surface. Alliances and betrayals, sabotage and deceit, destruction and slaughter. A battle royal where each group must fight with all their strength to survive."

Koizumi had a tired, cynical smile on his face.

"I do not believe that our theory is absolutely correct. However, I must accept it or I will be unable to continue in my current situation. I just happened to be initially placed on that side. I do not have the option of changing sides. A white pawn cannot switch to the black side."

Use Othello or shogi.

"It has nothing to do with you. Nor Suzumiya, for that matter. It is better that way. I especially hope that Suzumiya never learns about it. I do not wish to cause her grief. By my standards, Suzumiya has a lovable character. Of course, you do as well."

"Why are you telling me this?"

"Merely a slip of the tongue. There is no reason. Besides, I may merely be joking. Perhaps I'm being possessed by bizarre delusions. Or I'm simply trying to earn your sympathy. Whatever the case, it isn't amusing enough to discuss."

Yeah, definitely not amusing.

"I might as well tell you something else that isn't amusing. I've come up with a theory regarding why Mikuru Asahina . . . excuse me, Asahina was sent to accompany us. As you know,

Asahina appears to be a helpless, beautiful girl. I can understand why one would reflexively want to offer her help. You would probably accept everything she does in a positive way."

"What's wrong with that?"

It is the spiritual duty of normal people to help the weak and break the strong.

"Her role is to entice you. That is why Asahina's appearance and personality are the way they are. A timid, adorable girl who just happens to fit your tastes. You are the only person Suzumiya ever bothers listening to. Having a hold on you would be the optimal course of action."

I fell as silent as a deep-sea fish. I recalled what Asahina had said to me half a year ago. Not the present Asahina but the adult one who came from farther into the future. After summoning me with a letter, she said, "Don't get too close to me." Was she saying that because of her circumstances? Or was she expressing her personal feelings?

Koizumi took advantage of my silence to continue in a voice that sounded like an old Jomon Sugi was speaking.

"What if Asahina is merely playing the role of a clumsy girl and her true personality is something different? She judged that doing so would earn your sympathy. The same goes for her position as a poor little girl childish in appearance who has to suffer Suzumiya's unreasonable demands. It is all done to attract your attention."

This guy's seriously lost his sanity. I attempted to imitate Nagato's flat voice. "I'm sick of listening to your jokes."

Koizumi smiled a minuscule smile and spread his arms in an exaggerated fashion.

"Ah, forgive me. It would appear that I lack the ability to carry through a joke. I was lying. It was just a crazy setting I made up. I just felt like saying something serious. Did you think I really meant it? If that's the case, my acting skills aren't too shabby. I'm starting to feel confident about stepping onto a stage."

He continued after a grating chuckle. "My class will be performing Shakespeare. *Hamlet,* to be specific. I will be playing the role of Guildenstern."

"Never heard the name before. He's probably just a minor character, right?"

"Originally, that would be the case. However, as we progressed, we decided to switch to the Stoppard version. Which means I will have a much bigger role."

Good job. I didn't know there was another version of *Hamlet* besides Shakespeare's.

"Between Suzumiya's movie and this play, my schedule has been quite tight. It's a lot of pressure. If I appear to be mentally tired, that would be the reason why. I'm pretty confident that I would collapse if a closed space were to appear. That is another reason why I came to request your aid. To please stop the abnormal phenomena being caused by Suzumiya's movie."

The rational-conclusion thing? You mentioned the whole it-was-just-a-dream thing.

"I have to make Haruhi realize that everything in her movie is made up — right?"

"It must be a clear understanding. She's quite intelligent. She is well aware of the fact that her movie is fiction. However, she wishes that the world would become that way. We need her to clearly understand that it won't. Before the filming is over, preferably."

And after wishing me luck, Koizumi disappeared into the night. What was that? Did he come to shove the responsibility onto me? He already has a lot to deal with so I have to handle the rest? If that's the case, he's come to the wrong person. We're not talking about the joker in Old Maid here. You can't just push it around. And Haruhi Suzumiya isn't the fifty-third card here.

Not the trump card or ace in the hole either. And she's definitely not the maid.

"But still," I muttered.

I can't just ignore all of this. Nagato aside, Asahina and Koizumi look like they're almost out of hit points. The same may be true about the entire world for that matter, but I wouldn't know.

"That's a problem . . . I suppose."

What a pain. Damn. I'm pretty pooped myself.

I tried to come up with a plan. How to deal with Haruhi's delusions. A way to clearly make her understand that movie and reality are separate. What would be the method to make her accept such an obvious thing? It was all just a dream . . . or was there something else?

Only a little time remained before the cultural festival.

The next day, I made a suggestion to Haruhi. After some wrangling, she finally agreed to it.

"Okay!" Haruhi yelled loudly as she sounded the megaphone.

"Good work! We're done filming now! Everybody worked hard! Especially myself. Yep, I'm awesome! Great job!"

Upon hearing those words, waitress Asahina plopped down onto the ground. She looked relieved from the bottom of her heart. So relieved that it looked like she might cry. In fact, tears were flowing from her eyes. Haruhi apparently took those tears to mean that she had been overcome by emotion.

"Mikuru, it's too early to be crying. Save those tears for when you're awarded a Palme d'Or or an Oscar. We'll all be happy together!"

It was lunch break, and we were gathered on the roof of the school building. Tomorrow would be the cultural festival. We had been so short on time that we didn't even have time to calmly eat lunch.

The final battle between Mikuru and Yuki ended with the sudden awakening of some unknown power within Itsuki Koizumi and the usage of that convenient power to send Yuki flying into the deep reaches of space.

"This is perfect. We've made an incredible movie! If we take this to Hollywood, we'll have an avalanche of buyers. We should start by signing a contract with a skilled agent!"

Haruhi was cheerfully intent on going global. I had no idea who was going to watch this film, but the only selling point would be the leading actress, as nobody would want anything to do with the rest of the staff. In that case, I could tag along as Asahina's agent and promote her. I could probably make a little money that way. And while we were at it, maybe Haruhi could try to become a gravure idol or something? I was willing to send in her photographs and background without telling her.

"So it's finally over, huh?"

Koizumi smiled at me with a sunny face.

It's pretty aggravating, but he looked best when he had that free-of-charge smile on his face. I don't want to see a melancholic Koizumi. It would probably give me the creeps.

"But now that we're finished, it feels like it was all over in an instant. They say that time flies when you're having fun, but I wonder who was having fun in this case."

Beats me.

"Can I trust you to handle the rest? I can't think about anything besides our class play at the moment, since you aren't allowed to retake lines the way you can in movies."

Koizumi still had on his usual grin. He placed his hand on my shoulder and whispered in a soft voice, "One more thing. An expression of gratitude. From both my organization and myself."

And with that said, he left the roof. Nagato silently walked off after him with her usual blank expression.

Asahina was with Haruhi, who had one hand around Asahina's shoulders and the other pointing toward the ocean as they looked off into the distance.

"We're aiming for a Hollywood blockbuster!" she shouted. Feel free to point, but if you cross the ocean in that direction, you'll end up in Australia.

"Good grief," I muttered as I set the video camera down and sat. It may be over for Koizumi, Nagato, and Asahina. But this is only the beginning of the end for me. There's still something I have to do.

Somebody had to take the mass quantity of digital video I had filmed and somehow transform the accumulation of junk digital information into the semblance of a movie. And I'm pretty sure that I don't need to tell you to whom that task would fall.

It was Friday evening. Haruhi and I were the only people in the club room. The other three were working with their respective classes.

It was great that we'd finished shooting and all, but since the filming had taken so long, we barely had any time left to do the remaining tasks. As I replayed the footage I had loaded onto the computer, I came to the conclusion that we would have to turn this into a Mikuru Asahina promotional video clip. Very simple.

To be honest, I didn't even have the slightest pixel of an idea as to what kind of movie Haruhi was making to the very end. Are the waitress, Death-girl, and grinning boy on the monitor okay in the head? And naturally, there wasn't enough time left to search around for visual effects, and I didn't have that ability to begin with. We'd just have to screen the film without any processing or editing.

Haruhi grumbled, "We can't display an unfinished work! Do something about it!"

Is she talking to me?

"That's easy for you to say. The cultural festival's tomorrow and I'm already exhausted. Editing this thing to fit the story you made up was the best I could manage. I probably won't want to watch any movies for a while."

However, Haruhi excelled at crushing other people's opinions in an instant.

"Won't there be enough time with an all-nighter?"

And who's going to do that? Except I didn't say that. Since I was the only one there and Haruhi's ebony eyes were looking straight at me.

"You just have to stay overnight and finish the job."

And then Haruhi said something that left me utterly speechless.

"I'll help too."

In hindsight, Haruhi wasn't any help at all. She stood behind me for a while interfering, but it didn't even take an hour before she was sprawled on the table asleep. Damn. I should have filmed her sleeping. Then I could have put a still shot of that face after the ending credits rolled.

And I should mention that I also fell asleep soon after. By the time I opened my eyes, it was already morning and the keyboard was imprinted into half of my face.

Which means that there had been no point in staying overnight. The movie remained unfinished. I managed to cut and piece the thing into something under thirty minutes, but the result was pretty pathetic. Just a wreck filmed on a whim by a bunch of amateurs who didn't have the slightest clue about movies. I should have just defied Haruhi and only used the bunny Asahina shopping district commercials. When you consider that the objective of my editing was to match a story that didn't exist, which would be like spurring on a failure, the result would have to be something awful. In the end, there had been no dubbing or visual effects added. Just a garbage movie so bad it was laughable. I couldn't even show this to Taniguchi.

As I considered tossing the computer out the window, I squinted at the morning sunlight streaming in. I'd slept in an unnatural position, so my back was aching.

By the time Haruhi, who had woken up first, had shaken me awake, it was six thirty in the morning. Now that I think about it, this is the first time I've ever stayed overnight at school.

"Hey, how'd it go?"

Haruhi looked at the monitor over my shoulder. I had no choice but to move the mouse.

The film began playing.

". . . Huh?"

As I listened to Haruhi's soft cheering, I was astonished. A CG movie I had never made was magnificently displaying a moving title. At that point, *The Adventures of Mikuru Asahina Episode 00* began playing with a crappy story, dialogue you could barely hear, and shaky video; you could even hear the director yelling off the screen at times. However, the visual effects could be considered acceptable for a high school amateur film. Lasers were shooting from Asahina's eye and strange rays were shooting from Nagato's wand.

"Heheh —"

Haruhi was expressing her admiration.

"Not bad, huh? It feels a little lacking, but you did a good job."

It wasn't me. Unless another personality surfaced and did this while I was sleeping, there is no way I could ever accomplish this. Somebody else did it. Most likely candidate, Nagato. Possible contender, Koizumi. Out of the question, Asahina. Dark horse, somebody who hasn't made an appearance yet. Something like that.

We spent the next period of time silently appreciating our autonomously produced movie. I might have felt something different if I were watching this on a big screen instead of this small monitor.

The video on the display shifted to the last scene. Koizumi and Asahina were holding hands as they walked under cherry blossom trees in full bloom. The camera then panned up to show a blue sky. Cheap-sounding music began playing soon after as the staff roll began scrolling vertically.

And at the very end, Haruhi began narrating.

The idea I had devised was to force Haruhi to deliver this narration. I convinced her that the director herself should deliver these closing words as a bit of an inside joke.

They were the magic words that canceled everything that had occurred.

"This story is a work of fiction. There is no relation to any real people, organizations, events, or other names and phenomena. It's all made up. If anything seems familiar, it's just a coincidence. Oh, the commercials are an exception. Here's a shout-out to Ohmori Electronics and Yamatsuchi Model Shop! Give them lots of business! What? Say it again? This story is a work of fiction. There is no relation to any real people, organizations . . . Hey, Kyon. Why do I have to say this? Shouldn't it be obvious?"

EPILOGUE

The cultural festival had begun and I no longer had anything to do.

From a practical standpoint, I would have to say that people have the most fun during the preparation stage of an event. Once the event actually begins, everybody is hurrying around and time just zips by. The next thing you know, it's time to clean up. That's why I'll be lounging around until then. For the next two days at least, I can do whatever I want without anyone complaining.

By now, Haruhi, the only one who might complain, was probably standing by the school gate in her bunny-girl outfit, passing out flyers. At least until homeroom teacher Okabe and the executive committee show up to stop her. Well, I wonder how many she'll manage to pass out.

I left the club room and headed into the school grounds bustling with activity.

The alterations to reality we had feared had been quelled. That's what Koizumi claimed, and Nagato had confirmed it, so it must be true. I realized it when Shamisen stopped talking. He's as silent as Nagato now. It'd be kind of mean to kick him out at this point, so I'm planning on keeping him. My sister also seemed pretty happy about having a moving stuffed animal. I'll tell my family that "the former owner ended up moving to his travel destination."

The calico meows every now and then, which always makes me wonder if he's actually trying to say something else. Well, I suppose it doesn't matter.

Speaking of stuff that's no longer around, I hadn't been able to find a program in the cultural festival that would have featured that group of people I'd seen walking around in bizarre outfits.

I even checked the pamphlet issued by the executive committee and had a peek at all the classrooms that seemed remotely relevant (such as the drama club), but they weren't anywhere to be found. I wonder who those people were.

"Huh," I muttered for no reason before marching through the school building.

What if there were sliders wandering around our school? And the people in their world happened to wear fantasy-like clothing. Yeah, like what Nagato's been wearing.

Wouldn't that mean that Nagato had purposely walked around in that outfit from the beginning to trick Haruhi? As if to give Haruhi the impression that such costumes were merely part of a cultural festival.

Nagato never says anything so I can't be sure, but it's possible that she's engaged in some battle somewhere outside of my knowledge. She was awfully quiet this time. If she had to save the Earth from destruction or something, she would probably just silently do it. She might tell me if I asked, but it probably won't be anything she can communicate through words and I doubt I have the brains to understand her if she did.

That's why I decided to keep my mouth shut. Especially when Haruhi's around.

On a slightly related note, the SOS Brigade–produced movie was screened in the A/V room. Our film was screened with the Film Research Society's as a double feature. Haruhi basically forced the film society into doing it this way. It was the only classroom with a projector. The film society disapproved until the very last second, but there isn't a human on this planet who can go against a decision by Haruhi, so in the end Haruhi had her way and the cruddy commercial-loaded movie was screened.

By the way, the organization known as the SOS Brigade doesn't exist as far as the cultural festival executive committee is concerned, so there isn't an item labeled "The Adventures of Mikuru Asahina" on the cultural festival program. We should probably give up on placing first in the popularity poll. Any votes we get will probably end up going to the film society.

And on another slightly related note, remember the movie that had been broadcast late at night and had given Haruhi the idea of making a film in the first place? Upon further research, I discovered that the movie hadn't even won a Golden Globe. The movie was something called *Dake,* which had been screened at the Cannes Film Festival a fairly long time ago. Did she make some kind of mistake? Just to make sure, I rented it. I fell asleep after thirty minutes. Therefore, I was unable to determine if it was interesting or not. I'm planning on giving it another try before I return it.

I decided I might as well watch class 1-9's play.

Koizumi had a smile on his face the entire time he was acting his odd role, which met a rather stupid death at the end. About as stupid as Haruhi's film actually, but the audience seemed to enjoy it. Maybe I was just biased because the leading part had been played by Koizumi. And the fact that Koizumi looked like he was just being himself instead of acting definitely hurt.

When Koizumi came out in response to the applause after the curtain call, he looked at me and shut one eye. I left the classroom before his creepy wink could reach me. I figured I might as well check out Nagato's class, but by the time I reached the classroom holding the fortune-telling convention, there was already a long line. I peeked in to see a number of girls dressed in black costumes. Nagato's inorganically pale face was among them. She was saying something in a flat voice to a customer as she moved her hands above a crystal ball placed on the desk. Try to keep it to lost items and the like, Nagato.

The film and the trouble caused by the film were dealt with by making Haruhi realize that "it's all just fiction after all." However, you can't just say that the real world is fiction. You can't say that "people like that can't exist" when Haruhi, Asahina, Nagato, Koizumi, and I are all here. Eventually, we may all go our separate ways, but for now the SOS Brigade exists and the brigade chief and members are all together. That's the world as I know it. Or as Nagato put it, "For me, at least."

Well, what can I say? I have to wonder sometimes if this whole thing is just one big lie. Haruhi has no power. Asahina, Nagato, and Koizumi have just been putting on a grand show of lies. The white doves were painted. Shamisen was the result of ventriloquism or a hidden mike. The autumn cherry blossoms and the Miracle Mikuru Eye attack were all just tricks of some sort. Something like that.

Even if that were the case, I don't think I would really care.

"Guess there's no chance of that, though."

At any rate, none of that matters right now. Simple arithmetic will tell you that there's less strain on a person's head when we're all in this together instead of Haruhi and me being locked up somewhere by ourselves. The silver lining here would be that I'm not the only SOS Brigade member.

I'm the only normal one, though.

My eyes went to the clock in the classroom that was being used as a rest area, similar to 1-5.

Oops, this isn't the time to be sitting around. It's almost time. It'd be a waste not to use these coupons after they were given to me. And I'm also curious about what kind of costumes they'll be wearing.

I hurried to the spot where I would meet with Taniguchi and Kunikida to head to the yakisoba café where Asahina awaited.

AFTERWORD

As the convenience stores in my area have been going out of business one by one, I now have to walk approximately fifteen minutes to reach the nearest one, and there is a relatively large pond on the way that hosts migrating birds during winter.

I was passing by a while back and happened to see a male mallard duck drifting around the pond, even though it was already summer.

Well, I thought to myself, *what reason would a mallard have to part company with his brethren and isolate himself?* I pictured him being shocked after waking up one spring morning to discover that everyone was gone and he had been left behind and felt my heart ache as much as it would for the next person, but the other day, I went out late at night to buy something and saw the mallard quacking and splashing around in the middle of a river. It left me feeling relieved. So he's just an oddball.

Perhaps he was merely a rebellious duck like the humans who dislike moving around in groups for no particular reason. I daresay that when his brethren invited him to go north with them, he responded by saying, "No, I'll stay here. No real reason," and chose to deviate from the routine work of duck society. After all, he was weird enough to wander around in the middle of the night, so floating around in a pond by himself couldn't be a big deal. In fact, I surmised that he happened to prefer to be alone.

And so I convinced myself. But after a slight bit of research, I discovered that many migratory birds choose not to go north when spring comes. Basically, humans stop by the lake to feed them so they can live a comfortable life without having to worry about finding their own food. That would mean that he wasn't an oddball but rather a lazy bum, which shattered my arbitrary dream and left me dejected, which is why I wrote about it in this afterword. Of course, none of this matters to the mallard, as far as he is concerned.

Moving on to a different subject, there is a rumor that the next volume will be a compilation of short stories from *The Sneaker* (as of summer 2003) with the addition of a new original story. At the moment, I believe that the title will be *The Boredom of Haruhi Suzumiya,* but it is still subject to change. Of course, spending only three seconds to come up with the title *The Melancholy of Haruhi Suzumiya* has left me with a series title that doesn't seem quite right. I didn't expect this to become a series. I apologize.

On another note, I would like to thank the people who spent a great deal of time playing mah-jongg with me the other day. I would appreciate it if you could hold yourself back or show mercy . . . no, never mind.

* * *

Finally, I would like to express my gratitude to my editor, Mr. S, and the illustrator, Ms. Noizi Ito, along with everyone involved in the publication of this book, as well as all of the readers. I hope to see you again.

Nagaru Tanigawa

THE SIGH OF HARUHI SUZUMIYA

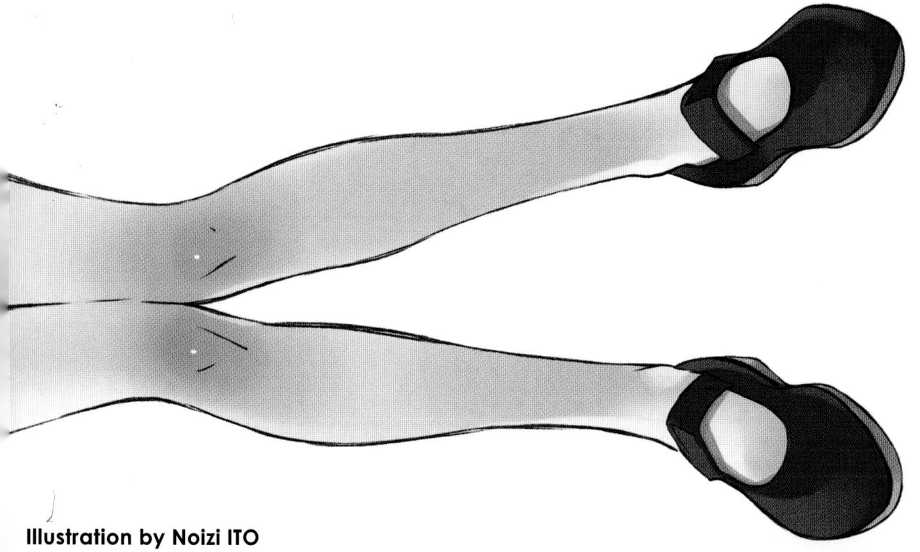

Illustration by Noizi ITO

TAP
THE SOS BRIGADE-STYLE
CULTURAL FESTIVAL MOVIE SCREENING
WHAT?

WE, THE SOS BRIGADE, WILL BE FILMING A MOVIE!

EH...?!
EEK!!

DANGER DRAWS
NEAR COMBAT
WAITRESS MIKURU!!

- DIRECTOR / PRODUCER / SCENARIO:
  HARUHI SUZUMIYA
- STARRING:
  MIKURU ASAHINA, ITSUKI KOIZUMI,
  YUKI NAGATO
- OTHER MENIAL TASKS:
  KYON

THE MOVIE EVERYBODY'S TALKING ABOUT THIS YEAR –
YOU'LL ABSOLUTELY REGRET MISSING THIS!

MIKURU

THE SIGH OF
HARUHI SUZUMIYA
NAGARU TANIGAWA
& NOIZI ITO